LAMBTON COUNTY LIBRARY. WYOMING ONTARIO

D0145387

RICHER THAN SIN

SIN TRILOGY BOOK ONE

MEGHAN
MARCH

NEW YORK TIMES BESTSELLING AUTHOR

WITHDRAWN

LAMBTON COUNTY LIBRARY, WYOMING, ONTARIO

LAMBTON COUNTY LIBRARY, WYOMING, ONTARIO

RICHER THAN SIN

Book One of the Sin Trilogy

Meghan March

Copyright © 2018 by Meghan March LLC

All rights reserved.

Editor: Pam Berehulke

Bulletproof Editing

www.bulletproofediting.com

Cover design: Letitia Hassar

R.B.A. Designs

www.rbadesigns.com

Cover photo: Wander Aguiar

http://www.wanderaguiar.com

No part of this book may be reproduced or transmitted in any form or by any means, electronic or mechanical, including photocopying, recording, or by any information storage and retrieval system without the written permission of the author, except for the use of brief quotations in a review.

This book is a work of fiction. Names, characters, places, and incidents are either products of the author's imagination or are used fictitiously. Any resemblance to actual persons, living or dead, events, or locales is entirely coincidental. The author acknowledges the trademarked status and trademark owners of various products referenced in this work of fiction, which have been used without permission. The publication/use of these trademarks is not authorized, associated with, or sponsored by the trademark owners.

Visit my website at www.meghanmarch.com

ABOUT THIS BOOK

A Riscoff and a Gable can never live happily ever after. Our family feud is the stuff of legends.

Ten years ago, Whitney Gable caught me off guard with her long legs and grab-you-by-the-balls blue eyes.

I didn't know or care what her name was.

Like any Riscoff man worth the family name, I went after what I wanted. And we burned like a flash fire until she married another man.

She hates me, and she should.

I objected on her wedding day.

Now she's home, with those same long legs and man-eater stare, but there's no ring on her finger.

They say a Riscoff and a Gable can never live happily ever after . . . but I'm not done with Whitney Gable.

I'll never be done with her.

Richer Than Sin is the first book in the Sin Trilogy.

PROLOGUE

LINCOLN

"I OBJECT."

Every head in the entire congregation swung toward the double doors I'd flung open.

My vision was fuzzy, no doubt from the two fifths of Scotch I'd used to try to drown out the fact that she was marrying someone else today.

Because a Gable and a Riscoff could never be together.

But that didn't mean I was going to watch Whitney Gable marry someone else and not say a goddamned word.

"You *asshole*. How *dare* you?" Whitney was dressed in white, looking like the perfect bride, aside from the militant look on her face as she stomped down the aisle toward me.

I might have miscalculated in my drunken haze.

"You can't marry him." I was pretty sure my words slurred, but I didn't care.

"I don't know why you think you get to have an opinion, but get the hell out of here."

"I can buy and sell him." More slurring.

Whitney's eyes burned with anger. "I. Don't. Care. Because *you can't buy me*."

Two sets of arms grabbed me from behind and dragged me back toward the doors.

"Don't do this—" My words were cut off as I was shoved down the front steps of the church.

"If you ever look at my sister again, I will fucking kill you myself. I don't care how much fucking money your family has." Asa Gable loomed over me, and I didn't doubt his promise, especially not while he was wearing his army dress uniform and green beret.

Next to him was the groom. The man who'd sold Whitney the biggest crock of shit I'd ever heard in my life. I'd told myself there was no way she'd ever go through with it. No way her brother would let her.

I was wrong. He'd let her marry anyone but a Riscoff.

The groom smirked but said nothing, then they both turned and marched up the steps.

If I weren't so fucking wasted, I'd go back in and try again.

He might be marrying her today, but I wasn't done with Whitney Gable.

I'd never be done with her.

LINCOLN

Ten years later – Present day

"TIME TO SHIT or get off the pot, boy. You can't keep her dangling after you forever. I'm not getting any younger, and you need to get started on the next generation. The Riscoff line must continue, and I'm sick of waiting."

My grandfather offers his unsolicited advice as my phone vibrates with a text on the table between us. We're having our regular morning meeting on his deck overlooking the gorge and the river.

"This isn't relevant to the conversation at hand." I slide my phone off the table and slip it into my pocket. Ignoring the message from the woman I've been seeing occasionally for the last few months, I flip open a file with a stack of documents needing Commodore's signature.

Business comes first. Last. Always. That's the Riscoff family way.

Any woman who spends time around me knows it, and that these meetings with my grandfather are sacrosanct. I may be the heir apparent to a multibillion-dollar empire, but

Commodore still officially holds the reins, and every decision I make has to be signed off on by him. Does it drive me fucking crazy? Yes. Do I have a choice? No, because that's family tradition. We preserve and protect the legacy at all costs. That's part of being the Riscoff heir.

"What is relevant, however, is you signing these documents so we can close the deal on these contract negotiations and make us another few hundred million before the end of the year."

I push the stack of resolutions in front of him and hold them down as the wind whipping off the river causes the pages to flap, threatening to carry them away. It was more convenient when he lived at the family estate, but that ended when he accused my mother of trying to poison him two years ago and moved out to this cabin overlooking the river. Now I have to haul my ass out here every day, over ten miles of winding roads up through the mountains, with shitty cell service.

Part of me wonders if he decided to buy this place because Magnus Gable, his lifelong sworn enemy, bought the falling-down place next door, and Commodore wanted to keep an eye on him.

Keep your enemies close. Commodore is Machiavellian enough that I wouldn't put anything past him.

I still don't know what to think about whether my mother was trying to poison him. Would she try to hasten his demise to force the company holdings to be passed down? I should be able to say no with certainty, and the fact that I can't says a lot about my family, and none of it good.

When there's billions of dollars at stake, no one's motives are without question, regardless of whether they share your blood, your name, or both.

Commodore's right hand, still tanned and capable, shakes just enough to be noticeable as he drags his finger across the pages, reading every single word. The other hand hangs over the side of his motorized chair, absently stroking the dark head of his Chesapeake Bay retriever, Goose. Just like his shotgun, the dog never leaves his side, except when Commodore yells, "Duck, duck, goose." The dog charges down the stairs to the river and vaults into the water to retrieve whatever Commodore shot.

Right now, the shotgun rests against the side of the chair beside me, most likely to menace Magnus Gable when the old men get riled up.

Commodore flips to the next page, reads it, and reaches out with his left hand for his Mont Blanc pen. Once he scrawls his signature on the page, he looks up at me. His brown eyes are still as sharp as my very first memory of him when I was four years old and he told me that my only job in life was to preserve and protect the family legacy.

"You did good on this deal. Proud of you, boy." He shoves the resolutions back into the folder and grabs the river rock he uses as a paperweight to keep the documents authorizing multimillion-dollar decisions from flying away.

"Thank you, sir." I reach for the documents.

"We're not done yet."

"Is there something else we need to discuss before I take this back to the office and make a shit-ton of money?"

"Damn right." Commodore leans back in his chair and crosses his arms over his barrel chest. His snow-white hair and thick beard barely move, even though the wind is picking up. "She's coming back."

My hand freezes in midair, hovering over the file as the old man studies my every move and reaction.

Machiavellian to the core.

5

"Excuse me?" I ask carefully, even though I heard him perfectly.

"You heard me. She's coming back, and I need to know if you're going to be able to keep your head this time."

I school my expression to show nothing. Another lesson from the old man.

"Who?" I ask, forcing as much nonchalance into my tone as possible. I voice the question to buy time as my brain spins with the information. There's no doubt who *she* is. There's only ever been one *she* for me.

Commodore unfolds his arms and leans forward, rests his elbows on the table, and interlocks his fingers. "Don't play that shit with me, boy. You know damn well who I'm talking about. Fuck the girl if you have to. Work her out of your system. Then move the hell on and get cracking on that next generation. I won't live forever, and I want to know that this company won't end up in Harrison's hands."

For all his billions of dollars, Commodore Riscoff still sounds like he just stepped off a navy ship when he's making sure there's no way to misinterpret him. My mind is going a million miles an hour, trying to make sense of what the hell is happening. Only one thing that he said matters.

She's coming back.

Whitney Gable . . . the only girl I ever wanted to see walk down the aisle in white.

And then she did. To someone else.

Ten years ago, she fucked my world six ways to Sunday when she walked into that bar . . .

LINCOLN

The past

I GOT CALLED home like a fucking dog. And like one of the obedient retrievers Commodore uses to fetch his birds, I came when I was called. That didn't mean I had to like it. What twenty-five-year-old man worth his salt packed up everything and skipped home when his grandfather snapped his fingers?

That's right. *Me.* It was what a good heir to a family fortune did.

But I didn't just do it for the money. No, I did it because Commodore had hammered the family motto into me since I was four years old—*Preserve and protect the legacy.* That's what Riscoffs did. We filled the family coffers with even more money than was there when we took the reins, and then passed it on to the next generation.

My father was doing a shitty job of living up to Commodore's rigorous standards, based on the reports I'd been getting in New York. Apparently, he spent more time with his mistresses than he did in the office. This last message made it clear that Commodore had had enough.

According to him, it was time for me to come back to Gable and pick up the slack.

I came, but I didn't have to like it. Just because I was an obedient heir didn't mean I wasn't a pissed-off one. Which explained why I was sitting in a hole-in-the-wall bar outside of town, glaring at the tequila in front of me.

I could handle whatever responsibilities Commodore threw at me, but I wasn't ready to come back to Gable. Not by a long shot. New York was in my blood, and I was climbing the ladder in a company where no one with my name sat in a corner office. I was proving myself and my worth.

Gable might be my home, but it had never been comfortable to live here. It was an enclave tucked into some of the most beautiful mountains I'd ever seen, but it was a town divided.

My family had seen to it over the years.

The Riscoff-Gable feud was the stuff of legends, and it wasn't dying anytime soon. Everyone had chosen sides, especially with the latest incident last month when Commodore bought the Gables' family farm at auction when they lost it for getting behind on taxes. Commodore didn't need or want it. He just enjoyed taking something from the Gables.

A day after the sale, the house and big barn burned to the ground. The cops didn't know if Commodore did it out of spite or if the Gables torched it because they couldn't handle the Riscoffs owning it.

I didn't fucking know the truth, and I didn't want to know. The only thing that mattered was that I couldn't go anywhere in this town without people looking at me and knowing exactly who I was, and half of them hated me. The anonymity I'd enjoyed in New York was stripped away the minute I stepped off the company jet.

I reached for the bottle of Patrón in front of me and poured a shot as the dull roar of the bar kicked up another notch.

It took me all of three days to find someplace I could sit and be pissed off without anyone looking twice at me. In my battered Mets cap, plain white T-shirt, and ripped jeans, no one gave a single shit who I was at Mo's. It was basically a shack favored by bikers heading up into the mountains. It was on the opposite fork of the road that headed to the family estate, a place I couldn't wait to escape the second I crossed the threshold. The estate was nothing but a reminder of family responsibility dictating the course of the rest of my life.

I was my own man, but with my grandfather calling the shots now, I was frustrated as hell.

Mo's was the perfect hideaway, and tonight I wanted to drink in peace while I tried to settle into the idea of accepting my fate. That would take a hell of a lot more tequila.

I was thinking about tossing back the liquor in front of me when the door opened and a gust of wind dragged everyone's attention toward the door, including mine.

Ho. Ly. Fuck.

Hair as black as the night. Lips as red as sin. A body built for a man's hands.

Jesus. Fuck.

I wasn't drunk, but the whole world seemed to slow down as her hair blew around her shoulders as she strode inside. It was like a goddamned photo-shoot pose—but she was completely oblivious to the accidental effect.

The dull roar of the bar quieted as every man inside seemed to drop his jaw at her arrival. It was like we were all waiting in anticipation for her to lift her head. She shoved something in her purse and looked up.

Are you fucking serious?

Her vivid blue eyes kicked me in the gut, followed by a sucker punch from the way she pursed her lips as she surveyed the bar like it was her kingdom. She personified the saying *walk in like you own the place.* With her shoulders back, tits out, and chin pointed up, she walked toward the bar with her disinterested stare firmly in place as she ignored every single man in the room.

A woman on a mission. *Fuck, that's hot.*

Confidence rolled off her as she took the seat two stools down from me and slapped a twenty on the bar. "Tequila. Straight up. ASAP."

I was right about the woman-on-a-mission part. Some poor fuck must have pissed her off, and the fire barely banked beneath all that smooth skin was the most tempting thing I'd experienced in ages. The punch of lust that hit me made my dick shift in my jeans, and I sat forward. I'd never been the kind of man who would let an opportunity like her pass me by.

I slid the bottle of Patrón down the bar toward her. "Here you go."

Those blue eyes grabbed me by the balls when she shifted her gaze toward me. "I'm not sleeping with you for buying me a drink."

I like her style. A smile crossed my face for the first time since I got the call from my grandfather that it was time to trot along home.

"That won't be why." I turned on my stool and held out a hand, driven by pure habit. "I'm—"

"Save it, city boy. I don't need to know your name to drink your tequila. I'm never going to see you again, anyway."

She saved me from giving up my identity, which made

her attitude even sexier—and made me want to prove her wrong. That was a special talent of mine.

"Why do you think I'm a city boy?"

She glanced down at my wrist. "Fancy watch." Her gaze dropped to my shoes. "And those aren't biker boots, hiking boots, or steel toes. You're not from around here."

She was wrong, but she was also right in a way. I was from Gable, but I wasn't raised here. My parents hired private tutors for me until I turned twelve, and then I was sent to boarding school. The same for my brother, but not my sister. My parents didn't think she needed a boarding school education because she could catch herself a husband in college. Thankfully, she was going to be a junior at Yale, and had more of a head for business than an eye for frat boys.

In the interest of maintaining my anonymity, I nodded in agreement before tilting my head to look at the worn heeled boots she was wearing with her short denim skirt.

"Do your boots mean you are from around here?"

Instead of answering my question, she stood up on the lower rung of the bar stool and reached over the bar to swipe a shot glass. The denim strained against her ass, and I knew I shouldn't look, but there was no way to fight that losing battle.

Jesus Christ, she's the full package.

As she sat, she splashed tequila out of the bottle until it filled her shot glass to the rim. "Born and raised, and all I want to do is get out of this town. I've had enough."

I watched as she tipped the tequila back, shooting it like an expert before smacking the glass back on the scarred wood. My attention stuck on the red lipstick print on the glass. I knew where I'd rather see those red lips.

When my dick stiffened against my zipper, I cut off that

line of thinking. I wasn't about to sit in a biker bar with a hard-on like a thirteen-year-old boy.

I dragged my gaze to her face, which was no hardship at all. Every time I looked at her, I noticed something different. The little freckle above her red lips this time.

Fucking Christ, she's gorgeous.

She raised an eyebrow, and I realized I'd been staring at her longer than I should have. I snapped myself out of her spell and tried to remember what the fuck we were talking about.

Oh, that's right. She wants the fuck out of Gable. That makes two of us, and I've only been here a few days.

"Where would you go?"

"Doesn't matter. I'm not getting out yet. I'm stuck." She opened her mouth to say something more, but then shook her head and snapped her mouth shut.

For some reason, I wanted to tell this girl—or by the looks of her, this woman—that I'd take her anywhere she wanted to go. But I didn't.

"You can't be truly stuck anywhere. You've got choices."

Her blue gaze landed on me again, and I swore someone sucked all the air out of the room. Never in my life had I felt chemistry like this.

"Maybe you have choices. But all my plans went to hell tonight. The only upside? I dropped a hundred eighty pounds of dead weight."

I was right in my initial assumption. Some asshole fucked up with this girl. *His loss. My gain.*

She reached for the neck of the bottle and poured another measure of tequila into her glass. When she lifted it to her lips this time, her gaze stayed locked on mine as she downed it. I lost the ability to form a complete sentence for the ten seconds it took for some douchebag to slide up next to her.

"You finally hear that asshole is fucking everything in sight? He dropped us like a bad habit when he got his chance. Shouldn't be surprised that he dropped you too when he's got every girl in LA trying to jump on his dick."

The woman glanced over her shoulder at the douchebag, her shoulders stiffening. "Fuck off, Dave."

"I'd rather fuck you, baby. Been waitin' years for my chance to tap your sweet ass."

"Not a chance in hell."

Clearly these two had some kind of history, and it wasn't my place to interfere. But when his hand shot out and wrapped around her elbow, I jumped off my stool.

"She didn't ask you to touch her, so keep your hands off."

Dave's attention shifted to me, and while he was distracted, Blue jumped off her seat and slammed the heels of both her hands hard against his chest.

"Don't ever touch me, you mother—" she started to yell, but went silent when Dave shoved her back and she tumbled against the bar stool.

Oh, hell no.

"You don't ever put your fucking hands on a woman, you piece of shit." I reached down and helped her to her feet before putting myself between her and Dave.

"Stay behind me." Something flashed in her gaze as it collided with mine, and she opened her mouth to say something, but I cut her off. "It's safer."

Glass shattered, and I spun around to see Dave grasping a broken beer bottle by the neck.

I might have grown up with money, but that didn't exempt me from having to defend myself if I wanted any respect in boarding school. I'd learned how to take a punch and how to deliver one by the time I was a teenager.

Dave waved the jagged glass at me, and I blocked with my forearm before landing a blow to his liver.

The broken bottle shattered when it hit the floor, and Dave dropped to his knees like a chump. Chairs scraped against the cement floor as the rest of the bar took notice, and bikers rose to their feet.

The other thing I learned? When to retreat.

I turned and faced the girl. "We're getting the fuck out of here."

Her head bobbed as she nodded, and her wide blue gaze darted over my shoulder as she slid her hand into mine. "Let's go."

I curled my fingers around hers and we made a break for the back door. She was on my heels as I shoved it open and led her out into the cool spring night air.

"I don't have a car."

"My truck's right here." I'd grabbed the keys to one of the utility trucks the estate kept in the garage.

The door of the bar smacked against the black cinderblock wall as someone burst through the door after us. I turned around, using my body to shield her once more, but I was too slow to protect my own face as his fist flew.

It glanced off my cheekbone, and I dropped her hand to shoot out with a right hook, catching him on his jaw. He staggered back as blood roared in my veins.

"That should not be attractive. *At all.*" Her husky voice filtered in through the adrenaline charging through my system. "But that was hot."

The guy came at me again, and I went for an uppercut. With a grunt, he dropped to his knees.

I stepped toward him, but a hand wrapped around my arm. Her gaze pleaded with mine.

"Let's go. He's not worth it. None of them are."

Walking away from him was the easiest decision I'd ever made. Two minutes later, we were in my truck, hauling ass out of the parking lot and spraying gravel.

"I'm so sorry. That's all my fault."

I glanced across the cab at her face, but it was hidden by darkness. Out here, there were no streetlights to illuminate the road, only my high beams as they cut through the night heading back toward town.

"You didn't ask him to put his hands on you, so I'd say it was Dave's fault. Whoever the hell he is. You want to tell me what that was about?"

"No. I don't want to think about it. Not tonight. Not ever. I just want to fucking forget about the whole mess."

"Where do you need me to drop you off?" I hated asking the question, because I didn't want to drop her off anywhere yet, especially on the off chance that it was her boyfriend's place because she hadn't moved out.

"No one has ever stood up for me. Never."

"It was nothing."

She turned in her seat. "Maybe to you, but not to me. It was everything."

When her seat belt clicked and retracted, I glanced over at her. "What are you doing?"

She scooted over to the middle of the bench seat. "Saying thank you." Her lips pressed against my cheek.

If I dropped her off tonight, I knew I'd never see her again, and something in my gut railed at the thought.

There was only one fucking place I wanted her to go—with me. And not to the estate. Never to the fucking estate. That place sucked the life out of everything the minute you walked in the door.

I spotted a turnoff up ahead and pulled over to the side of the road. When I flipped on the dome light, her chest was rising and falling, and her blue gaze was locked on me.

My blood, already raging from the fight, heated another hundred degrees. I saw the answering lust in her expression. She wanted me. I had enough experience to recognize it when I saw it.

She says she wants to forget? I can think of the perfect way to make that happen.

I turned in my seat. "You want to thank me, you kiss me right."

Her eyes widened, the pupils dilating as she inhaled sharply. For a moment, I wondered if I pushed too hard, too fast, but instead of sliding back to her side of the truck, she scooted closer.

"I don't normally do this. It probably makes me easy, but—"

"This doesn't make you anything but perfect." I barely recognized the growl in my voice as I gripped her by the hips and hauled her onto my lap.

Her mouth crushed against mine with more enthusiasm than skill, and something about that made it even hotter. I buried a hand in her hair and kept the other clamped around her hip as I took control of the kiss, turning her head so I could get deeper. Take more. Taste more.

She was fire and heat and spice. Tasted like trouble. And I wanted it all.

She knocked the hat off my head and grasped the back of my neck, kissing me with hunger I hadn't felt in years.

"I want you."

I forced myself to pull back at the words she breathed. I didn't even know this girl's name. I couldn't fuck her in my truck.

Her gaze sharpened on me. "Don't go backing down on me now, city boy."

"Not here. We can both do better."

I forced myself to lift her off my lap, but I didn't let her go far. I curled my arm around her and tucked her next to me, ducking my head to steal another taste of her lips.

Fuck, she's like a drug.

I had to have her.

"I know where we can go."

THE RIDE to the cabin was short, and we were lucky as hell I managed to keep the truck on the road rather than putting it in a ditch, because I was so distracted by the girl next to me.

She was quiet, but her hand hadn't left my thigh, and the pads of her fingers might as well have burned holes through my jeans with the heat of just her touch.

When I pulled up in front of the small cabin, she turned to look at me, indecision lining her features.

"I need you to know something, and I need to know something from you before we go in there."

As much as it would kill me for her to change her mind, I nodded, preparing myself to take her home instead.

"I don't do this. I know that's what girls who do this kinda thing say, but I need you to believe me when I say that's the honest truth." The vehemence in her tone underscored just how serious this was to her. "I'm not a whore or a slut or easy."

"Stop," I told her. "Just stop."

Her red lips closed and she swallowed.

"I want you," I said. "I wanted you the second you walked in that door. Why the fuck would I think badly of you when I'm in the same boat? No judgment necessary, okay? I believe you."

She studied my face like she wasn't sure if I was blowing smoke up her ass, and I truly wasn't. Double standards were alive and well, but my perspective was a little different on the matter, given my father's behavior.

"Okay," she said with a nod.

"Now, what do you need to know about me?"

She stayed quiet.

"Ask away. Whatever you need."

"You're not a serial killer, are you?" Her brow furrowed, and I had a feeling her question was completely serious.

"No." I shook my head as my laugh echoed in the cabin of the truck.

"Because if you are, I promise I'll come back and haunt you for the rest of your life if you kill me. I might be little, but I'll be full of rage."

"I believe you," I told her, the first smile in days tugging at the corners of my mouth. "I promise I'm not a serial killer. Shot a few deer in my day, and that's it. You've got no reason to believe me, but you're safe. Nothing is happening tonight that you don't want or ask for."

Her hesitation told me more than her words ever could. This was out of character for her. She didn't go home with random guys from the bar. I was guessing, if she hadn't broken up with her boyfriend, she probably wouldn't have been at the bar.

"Good. I've been the queen of bad decisions in my life, and I don't want this to be one of them."

"You're good. I give you my word as a—" I almost said *Riscoff*, but I stopped short.

Her brows went up. "Your word as what?"

"A man who would've been beaten for disrespecting a woman."

It was the first thing that came to mind, and it was absolutely true. Commodore would kill me, and then my mother would bury me in the garden. That was one thing they both agreed on.

She looked out the windshield at the cabin, lit up by the brights of the truck. "This your place?"

I nodded and killed the engine. In the interest of keeping my identity out of the conversation, I didn't tell her that it was a hunting cabin that had been in the family for decades. It was normal, not too over-the-top, and I'd always been more comfortable here than at the estate.

I didn't sense hesitation in her tone, but I still wanted to be sure she was on board as I pulled the keys out of the ignition. "You want to change your mind?"

She shook her head with a smile, and my body buzzed like I'd taken a hit of something strong.

Thank God. But I didn't say that.

Instead, I said, "You're something else, Blue." I didn't know why I gave her a nickname, but it rolled off my tongue so easily.

"I'm nobody," she said as she looked away. "But tonight, I want to forget that."

I reached out and stroked her cheek with my thumb. "You're not nobody. I don't need to know your name to know that. But tonight, I'll make you forget everything that sent you into that bar, if you want."

Her gaze lifted to mine. "That's exactly what I want. Starting right now." She turned toward me and threw a leg over, her skirt rolling up her thighs as she straddled my lap again. Her body practically vibrated with need.

Never in my life had a woman wanted me this badly without knowing who I was.

Panties usually flew when they find out my last name, but this girl lit up for *me.* Just me. That knowledge was more potent than an entire bottle of tequila.

Our lips collided, and her kiss was filled with hunger and desperation. I gave it right back to her. Whatever she was feeling, I was feeding off it, and it amplified everything.

I finally tore my mouth away. "We gotta get inside. I'm not fucking you for the first time in this truck. Not happening."

She opened her mouth to argue, but my hand was already on the handle. I maneuvered us out of the cab and lifted her so I could carry her inside.

"You might be a city boy, but you don't act like it." Her hands gripped my shoulders.

A smile tugged at my lips as I stopped at the door and let her slide down my body until her feet hit the ground. There was no way she could miss the hard bulge in my jeans from the way she'd climbed on me in the truck.

"Glad you approve."

As I faced the door, I realized I didn't have a fucking key. *But I do know where the spare is hidden.*

"Hold on one sec." I took a few steps to the side and lifted the moss-covered rock directly below the middle window.

"Lost your key?"

"It's somewhere, and I'm not taking the time to hunt for it." It wasn't exactly a lie. I knew exactly where the keys were, but I wasn't going back to the estate to get one.

"Fair enough."

When the unlocked door swung open, I lifted her into my arms again, carrying her over the threshold before kicking it shut behind us. Instead of flipping on the living room lights, I took her to the bedroom and shut the door before lowering her carefully to her feet.

She stood before me.

"You changing your mind?"

She shook her head as she pressed her palms to my chest. "Didn't expect a city boy to be so hard."

"Honey, you have no idea." I stepped forward, sliding one knee between her slightly spread legs. I pressed my palm to the small of her back and pulled her against me so she could feel exactly how hard I was.

Her gaze heated, even as indecision warred on her face.

"Nothing happens that you don't want."

"But what if I want it all?"

"Then that's what you'll get."

I cupped her ass and spun her around so her back was to the bed. I flexed, lifting her onto the bed before following her down and letting some of my weight rest against her.

Her body cradled mine, and all I could think was *I want more.*

More contact. More skin. More of those burning blue eyes studying my face.

She reached up and her fingers skated along my cheekbone. "You got hurt."

"I only feel you." My dick hardened as it rocked against her center.

"I wasn't kidding when I said I've never done this before," she blurted, and I jerked my head back.

"You're a virgin?" My body stilled.

"No. No. I mean . . . I've never had a one-night stand." She turned her head to the side like she didn't want to look at me. "God, that sounds cliché."

I used two fingers to gently guide her gaze back to mine. "Remember what I said? No judgment. I mean it. I

21

want you more than I remember wanting another woman ever."

Heat flared in those blue eyes again. "Then maybe we should stop with all the talking."

This girl, whoever the hell she might be, was fire and innocence mixed together in the most dangerous way possible.

My protective instincts warred with my need to strip her and sink my cock inside her. Every feeling she drew from me was so new and different. I didn't know what the hell was happening tonight, but I believed she and I were both in that bar, at the same time, in the same place, for a reason.

And whatever that reason was, it brought us here. I wasn't going to waste that chance.

I cradled her head and took her lips again. They were soft and smooth, and she kissed like she was struggling to hold back her hunger. I couldn't wait to build it until she had no choice but to explode.

I was going to make this the best night of her life. She might forget what took her into that bar, but she would never forget me. And if we were remotely as explosive together as I thought we were going to be, then this wouldn't be a one-time thing. That would give me one real reason to smile about being back in this town.

Her hands tugged at my shirt, and we broke apart so she could strip it over my head.

"You're beautiful," she said, her voice catching when she stared at my chest.

"No, that's you."

Her blue eyes pierced through me. All the things weighing on me—the expectations, the pressure—disappeared like they'd never existed. There was nothing but her and me and this night.

We tore each other's clothes off like we were half-crazy, and when I slipped off her shirt to uncover her gorgeous tits and perfect nipples, my dick pulsed against my jeans, straining to be inside her.

As much as I wanted to take her hard and fast, I wanted to take care with her. She'd been fucked over by some guy, and I wasn't about to do the same thing to her.

I pulled off her skirt and breathed in the scent of her. "You're soaked, aren't you, Blue?"

"It's your fault. You did it. I—"

"What?"

"I've never . . . not like this. So fast. So . . . everything."

Her disjointed words sent a charge of possession and triumph through me. Whatever my goal was when I brought her through the door, it changed. I wanted her addicted to me. Dying for me. I wanted to be the only person who could make her feel this way.

And she doesn't even know my name.

It was a headier feeling than anyone else would ever understand, and to me it was the ultimate aphrodisiac. I didn't need her name to know that I wanted her more than I'd ever wanted anyone. Maybe it was the adrenaline. Maybe it was the need for me to claim something in this town as my own. Whatever it was, it didn't matter.

I moved down her body and peeled off her panties. She arched against me, and I breathed in her scent.

She hadn't lied. She was soaked, and from the way she was lifting her hips, she was dying for this as badly as I was.

How long has it been since someone took care of her?

Immediately, I blocked out the question before my brain could think about the answer. However long it had been, she wouldn't remember anyone before me.

Her nails dug into my shoulders as my thumb skated over

the prettiest pussy lips I'd ever seen. Shivers rippled through her body.

"So responsive. So wet. So fucking hot."

She opened her mouth to reply, but all she managed was a mewl. At least until I lowered my head and swiped my tongue through her sweet wetness.

"Oh God. Do that again."

A sneaking suspicion formed in my brain that while this girl might not be a virgin, and while she did come home with me after knowing me for all of a half hour, she wasn't lying when she said she didn't do things like this.

That just made it more imperative that I make tonight unforgettable.

Her body responded, muscles clenching and head rocking, as I ate her like she was my last meal. She writhed against my mouth, moaning until her screams filled the cabin and a burst of tart wetness hit my tongue.

Fucking incredible.

I lifted up, dragging a finger through her slick folds, loving the way her body trembled when I touched her. "I want you. Right now."

Her gaze locked with mine, and she spread her legs the barest inch. "What are you waiting for?"

Her innocence mixed with her bold words was the most intoxicating combination. I didn't have a chance in hell at being able to resist, even if I wanted to.

I pushed off the bed and undid the button of my jeans. Her eyes widened when my cock sprang free.

"Holy shit."

Her hushed voice sounded like a prayer, and it made me feel like the luckiest man alive. I wrapped my palm around my dick and gave it a rough tug. Her blue eyes locked on the tip, and as badly as I wanted those red lips wrapped around it, I wanted to be inside her more.

I pulled out my wallet and found a condom. I tore it open with my teeth, thanking God that it was intact. She watched my every movement as I rolled it on, and part of me wanted to tell her she could help. Instead, I reveled in the heat blazing from her eyes that was evenly matched by her body.

"You ready?"

With a nod, she whispered, "Hurry."

Thank God.

Once the condom was secure, I lowered myself over her, loving the feel of her soft curves under me. Nothing like those stick figures dressed in solid black that filled the clubs in New York. She gripped my shoulders, and her hips bucked against my dick like they were trying to force it inside.

My jaw clenched, and my control felt like it was about to snap as I notched the head against her opening. "No going back from this, Blue."

"I don't want to go back. I want this."

As soon as the last syllable left her mouth, I plunged inside.

My brain went completely blank. The feel of her tight, wet heat robbed me of every memory of sex before and replaced it with *her*. Her body clamped down on mine before releasing and letting me slide in to the hilt.

She was no virgin, but she might as well be one. A growl rumbled from my throat at the possessive instincts she spawned in me.

Her fingernails dug into my shoulders. "I didn't know it could feel this good."

I didn't know what kind of piece of shit was fucking her before, but she wouldn't remember him come morning.

Neither of us would remember what it was like to be with anyone else, if I fucked her the way I planned.

I pulled back and pushed forward, and her hips rose to meet me as I thrust inside. Over and over, I pushed into her until she thrashed and screamed. It took everything I had not to stop. Not to lose my rhythm. I kept fucking her as her inner muscles clamped down, and she came so hard that I almost did too.

"Oh my God!"

She went limp, and I finally let myself go. My release was ripped straight from my balls, and with my cock still pumping inside her, I stared down at her.

What the fuck just happened? What kind of spell did this girl weave over me?

And more importantly . . . *Who is she?*

I had to know.

Because if someone told me she was planted in that bar tonight to entrap me into doing whatever I could to have another taste of her, I'd believe him.

I'd had plenty of good sex. Great sex. But Jesus fucking Christ, nothing like this. Everything else paled in comparison.

Her body was limp when I pulled out, and I couldn't help but smile. Made a man feel fucking good when the orgasm he gave a girl knocked her out.

My body and brain, both worn down from the past few days of running the gauntlet, wanted one thing before I could have her again—sleep.

I took care of the condom before tucking her under the covers and curling my body around her.

She wasn't leaving tomorrow until I knew her name and how soon I was going to see her again.

Maybe I was crazy, but this felt a whole fucking lot like fate.

I reached for her twice in the night, expecting the sex to be nothing like the first time, but I was wrong.

It was even better.

Her body was attuned to mine. She rode me until I came, and it was the most beautiful thing I'd ever seen. The next time, I took her from behind, one hand buried in her hair, my possessive instincts out of control when it came to this girl.

I didn't need to know her name to know she was meant to be mine.

I drifted off to sleep one more time, my fingers tangled in her hair.

WHEN I OPENED my eyes a few hours later, the bed was empty. I shot straight up and looked around.

She was gone.

I did not fucking imagine last night.

Then I heard boards creak out in the living room.

Fuck, she's sneaking out.

Not only was I not letting her leave without getting her name, but she had no way to get home.

I bolted out of bed, not bothering with my jeans, and reached the living room. "Hey—"

She whipped around from where she was standing, fully dressed, by the front door. But she wasn't looking at the door. No, she was staring at a picture below a trophy mount and an antique rifle.

A picture of me, my father, and my grandfather.

Instead of a sated smile, her face was the picture of horror.

"Are you okay?"

She backed away, edging toward the door, and tripped over one of her boots as she reached for the handle.

"You . . . you're . . . Lincoln Riscoff. Aren't you?" Her expression was echoed by the horrified tone of her voice.

No woman had ever looked at me like that before. Normally when they found out my name, they were on me faster than I could fend off.

My chin went up. "Yeah. So?"

"*Shit.*" She reached down and grabbed her boots before ripping the door open.

She was already partway down the drive before I hit the front porch.

"Wait!"

She gave me a backward glance and stumbled, dropping one of her boots. She didn't even stop to pick it up. She just bolted.

Fuck.

WHITNEY

Present day

TEN YEARS. That's how long it's been since I last saw the WELCOME TO GABLE sign as I drove away as a newlywed in the back of a limo filled with regrets.

Since then, I can't say how many times I've thought about making my return. A hundred? A thousand? Somewhere in between, most likely. I've pictured myself in a fancy sports car with my hair tucked into a scarf like I was Grace Kelly, or maybe in a chauffeur-driven SUV.

Not once in those ten years did I think I'd be coming back to town on a Greyhound bus.

The woman next to me snores so loudly, she wakes herself up. Her head jerks from side to side as she wipes drool from the corner of her mustache.

"What'd I miss?" She leans over me to look out the window as we approach the bus station.

"Nothing," I reply as I pull my baseball cap over my eyes and readjust my sunglasses to hopefully cover my black eye where the makeup is wearing off. Thankfully, she hasn't recognized me. I'm hoping my iffy luck will hold until I'm off this bus, and she won't have a clue who she sat next to on this long ride from LA.

When I left in the back of that limo, only one of us was famous then—Ricky Rango, rising rock star who was destined to become a rock god. Now he's six feet under, and I'm the famous one because I'm the Black Widow who killed him. Or so they say.

I know the truth, but no one else cares about anything so mundane as that. The fall from wife of a rock god to the most hated woman in America has been a rocky one, and to be honest, I'm lucky I made it out of LA alive.

The Greyhound's brakes squeal as it slows to a stop, changing the direction of my thoughts. It's time to stop thinking about what I'm running from and put it behind me, if that's even possible. I'm ready to think about what I'm running *toward*.

I just never thought I'd be running toward Gable, the place I spent so many years desperate to leave. But now everything has changed. All I want is a simple, quiet life. Something normal. Away from the paparazzi and accusations. Away from the guilt and fear. I'm hoping Gable can be my safe haven, but I'm also not holding my breath.

I glance out the window, expecting the old wooden train depot, but we're on the wrong side of town for that. Ahead is a glass structure that looks much too new to be part of Gable's historic charm, but sure enough, it has RISCOFF MEMORIAL BUS TERMINAL in large letters on the side.

Riscoff. That's one major reason I don't know if I'll ever find peace here.

As soon as we hit the city limits a few minutes ago, my heart jacked up to aerobic rates and my skin started feeling too tight for my body. It was like every part of me knew we were in close proximity to *him*.

I force my breathing to slow and try to look at the name without feeling anything.

Fail.

So instead, I glare at it, like that's going to help me find some inner strength that I haven't already used up defending myself against the press and angry fans. Of course the bus terminal is named after their family. It would match everything else in this town emblazoned with the Riscoff name.

The hospital that's probably only a mile from here. The courthouse that takes up one side of the town square. Then there's Riscoff Bank and Trust two blocks over, near the Riscoff Art Gallery. And of course, there's the granddaddy of them all on the other side of the river from downtown, Riscoff Timber.

The only thing that doesn't have their name is the town itself. I'm pretty sure my ancestors are still smiling in their graves about snaring that honor—right before they jumped the Riscoffs' gold claim and started a feud that's lasted over 170 years. During that time, both families have proven over and over how capable they are of sustaining such hate and bitterness.

I did my part too, and I'm not proud of it.

I wait my turn, specifically for the woman beside me to move, so I can haul my ass off the bus. The driver unearths my luggage from underneath and leaves it on the sidewalk near the glass-fronted bus station. The bus rumbles to life again, and I watch as it rolls away. I'm left surrounded by the sum total remains of my former life, in the form of ridiculously overpriced Louis Vuitton luggage, while I wait for my chronically-late-from-birth cousin to come get me.

If it hadn't been for Cricket begging me to come back to Gable, I probably would have stayed on the bus all the way to Canada. I hear they're friendly up there . . . unless they're Ricky Rango fans. At least in Gable, there's no love lost for the home-town boy who made good. He managed to burn that bridge when he went off during a concert, ripping this whole town a new one.

"Ohhh, baby! Look at that sexy thing just waiting on a ride. You wanna come on up with me, girl?"

If the catcall had come from a man, I would have tensed and prepared to bolt, but no. That's a voice I'd recognize even if it had been eighty years since I'd been home instead of ten.

For the first time in months, a genuine smile stretches my lips. "You know I don't get into a stranger's van unless someone offers me candy first."

"Well, get up here, little girl. I've got sugar for you." Cricket puts the van in park and hops out, running around the front of the giant Econoline. "Jesus Christ, you look just like a real celebrity—who forgot to tell her chauffeur where to pick her up."

I rush to meet her. We collide in a hug. "I thought you were my chauffeur. And early too. I was prepared to wait an hour for Cricket Time."

My cousin smells exactly the same as the last time I saw her—like pot smoke, coconut, and sunshine.

"God, I missed you, girl. It's been way too fucking long."

I pull back. Her tawny eyes dance, and her dark brown hair is braided around the crown of her head like she's a perfect flower child. And she's right.

My heart squeezes at her smiling face. I've missed her too. I shouldn't have stayed away so long.

"I know. I'm sorry. I'm so sorry—"

Cricket rolls her eyes. "Shush. You're here now. That's what matters. And you're going to be my maid of honor!"

My stomach clenches, and I'm sure my face looks like I just stepped on a downed power line."Wh-what?"

Cricket playfully shoves my shoulder. "You knew I wanted you home for my wedding. What makes you think I wouldn't want you to be my best bitch?"

"The fact that you have a twin sister?"

Cricket's eye-roll game steps up a notch. "She's not my best bitch, though. She's just a bitch."

I haven't seen Karma in ten years. She never came to LA or met me at any of Ricky's concerts when I traveled with him. I assumed she was mad I missed the birth of her daughters, but Karma was born pissed off, so it's hard to tell.

"I still can't believe you're getting married." I study my cousin, who is exactly one year younger than me and looks every bit the free spirit she's always been. Her flowy shirt is probably hemp, and her cut-off shorts are likely ones she stole from me when she was sixteen years old. "You swore you'd only ever love God, nature, and your family."

"That was until I got the good dick. Now I gotta put a ring on it so I can make sure I've got that shit locked down for life."

My smile widens so far it hurts my cheeks, and real laughter rings from between my lips. "Good God, Cricket. I've missed you like crazy."

"Well, obviously. None of those fake bitches in LA could hold a candle to your best girl. We're blood, baby. It don't get better than that."

She hugs me again, and I squeeze tight like she might slip away and I'd lose the one good thing that's happened to me in years. When we finally separate, I pull my sunglasses off to catch the tears gathering on my lids.

Cricket tilts her head to the side. "Please tell me you got mugged. Because what the fuck, Whitney?"

33

I wince as I touch the tender skin on the right side of my face, and then quickly slip the giant shades back on. "Angry fan. Got through security and went a little crazy."

All peace and joy flees Cricket's expression. "I'm going to kill that limp-dick motherfucker. And the fan who did this."

There's no doubt she's talking about Ricky first.

"That's going to be a little tricky." I try to keep humor in my tone, but it falls flat. "Considering he's already dead."

"Fucker deserves to be brought back to life and run over by a truck repeatedly for what he did to you."

I don't want to think about the message Ricky posted on his fan page hours before that fatal dose hit his bloodstream. He doesn't get to ruin my reunion with my cousin. He doesn't get to ruin anything else in my life ever again.

"Can we get out of here?" I glance up at the glass building and the name looming over me. "As much as I like hanging out at bus terminals . . ."

"Damn right. Besides, we've got way too much to catch up on, and that's best saved for non-bus-station conversations. I've got all the good-dick stories to tell you."

With a smile back on my face, despite memories from Gable and LA hounding me, Cricket and I load everything I own in the entire world into the back of her conversion van—after she folds up the bed and moves a bottle of lube.

When I stare at it wide-eyed, she just laughs as we climb up into the burgundy cloth captain's chairs that I'm pretty sure might swivel.

"What? If they didn't want people to fuck in these, they wouldn't have put beds in the back. Besides, Hunter works all the time, and I like to make sure I don't miss out on my chance to get me some. I like multiple orgasms, and he can make this baby rock and roll. I know you haven't seen him in years, but let me tell you—"

I hold up a hand. "Wait. Hunter who?"

Cricket, the sneaky ho who withheld the name of her groom in all our conversations because she wanted to tell me in person, smiles wide. "Hunter Havalin. He's the lucky man who snagged me."

My jaw hangs slack and my eyes feel like they're about to bug out of my head. Hunter Havalin is the only son of one of Gable's other affluent families. The Havalins aren't Riscoff rich, but they're still loaded.

I try to picture Cricket the free spirit, Ms. One with the World who eschews money and privilege, marrying a guy who probably knows every inch of the country club. My cousin is everything that is the exact opposite of Hunter Havalin. He was a senior when I was in middle school, and *every* girl had a crush on him, but he only dated girls from the private school one city over.

"*Are you serious?*" I finally manage to blink. Cricket's giant smile is the only thing keeping me from asking her if she had a bad trip she didn't tell me about.

Her glow fades at my shocked tone. "See? *This* is why I didn't tell you. I knew if you knew that I was marrying Lincoln Riscoff's best friend, you'd *never* come home."

I jerk back in my seat like I just got hit with a wrecking ball. First, because she spoke the name that is not to be spoken, and second, because *I didn't know they were friends*.

"What?" The word comes out between a cough and a squeak.

"Whit, please. Do not freak out. It's not like Lincoln is the best man or something. I would never put you in that position. He's way too busy for that, anyway."

I don't know what to say to her. Lincoln Riscoff is the one

person I plan to avoid for the rest of my time on planet earth, and definitely for as long as I'm in Gable. Which, if the Riscoffs have anything to say about it, may not be long.

"So," Cricket says, glossing over the information bomb she just dropped on me. "Where do you want to go first? Home, or Cocko Taco for the Taco Tuesday special? Be warned, Mom won't be out of work yet, and Karma is definitely home because unless she's doing something with her girls, she never steps away from her freaking computer and reality TV."

Blood is blood, but if Cricket, the most loving and forgiving person I've ever met, still can't handle her sister's attitude, I'm in no hurry to see my other cousin.

"Taco Tuesday it is."

Cricket nods and fires up the van. "That's my girl."

I'm not sure if she's talking about me or the van, but it doesn't matter, because she's swinging out of the parking lot and narrowly misses a little red Audi convertible. The blonde in the Audi lays on the horn and flips up her finger before flooring it and taking off at a speed the van has no prayer of reaching.

"Whore," Cricket says under her breath.

"Who was that?"

The rear end of the Audi disappears as it careens around a corner, its tires almost clipping a curb. At this point, I'm not sure who's the worse driver, her or my cousin.

Cricket shoots me a sideways glance. "You don't want to know."

My stomach, which is already knotted into a ball, twists tighter in anticipation.

"Why?"

My cousin's gaze slides back to the road. "That's Maren Higgins. She's . . . well, let's just say you don't want to talk about it—and neither do I—because we both have a reason to run her over on purpose. I like to refer to her as Cuntcake McWhoreson because it makes me feel better about myself and life in general."

"What did she do to you?" I don't even want to entertain the thought of why I might have a reason to run her over. "Because you know I'll still cut a bitch."

Cricket's grin comes back. "I know you will. That's why I'm glad to have you home. Maren is . . . Well, let's just say there's a special place in hell reserved for women who think they deserve to have a man who's already taken, and she's one of them."

"She tried to steal Hunter?"

Cricket nods. "They went out on two dates a few years ago, and then she set her sights on . . ."

Cricket stops before she says the name, and I tense because there's only one person whose name I told her not to mention.

"Well, she set her sights on a bigger target and has been slobbering after him ever since. But, because she's a Cuntcake McWhoreson, as soon as Hunter and I went public about our thing, she came running back because she was afraid of losing what she thought was a sure bet. Unlike her other option, who has basically made zero signs of ever committing, regardless of how much his family would love him to start popping out the next generation of rich kids."

"So . . . what did you do?"

"Told her I knew a voodoo priestess who would curse her to marrying a man with no money and no teeth. She backed off, but I don't trust her as far as I can see her. Apparently, she's also got a golden twat, because she's got half the guys in town under her spell."

I already hate her. I've never seen anything but her middle

finger and her convertible, but considering she tried to steal my cousin's man—and only for that reason—I'd bury her body for Cricket without question.

I tell myself I don't give a damn who she has under her spell or who wants her to use her golden twat to pop out an heir. *I'm a thirty-one-year-old broke, bitter widow, and I don't have room in my life for another man.*

I came back to Gable to be close to Cricket and my aunt Jackie, and that's it. I want to find a job and live a normal, quiet life, and stay out of the public eye. I don't need people like Cuntcake McWhoreson popping up and causing problems, because I had enough of that with my *friends* in LA who sold me out to the tabloids by giving them bullshit information about my broken marriage with Ricky.

My goals are simple now. Be happy. Keep the people I love close. Stay out of the press.

There's no room for wasting a single thought on the man who shall not be named. None at all.

Even if I never get the good dick for the rest of my life. I'll consider it penance for all the destruction I've left in my wake.

Except nothing could be that easy.

"There's Hunter's truck!" Cricket veers into oncoming traffic as she hangs her body out the window and waves at a fancy dark green pickup truck parked on the other side of Bridge Street.

"Jesus Christ, Cricket!"

I grab the wheel and jerk it toward the right so we don't hit the black sedan blaring its horn. My sunglasses go flying toward the dash, and I catch sight of Hunter Havalin on the sidewalk beside his truck.

And standing next to him, because I'm cursed, is Lincoln Riscoff.

WHITNEY

The past

WASHING windows was my least favorite of all the cleaning tasks on my to-do list. I would rather clean toilets from dawn till dusk if it meant I never had to wash another window. My arms ached from making sure the floor-to-ceiling panes of the boutique were spotless. Not to mention the other parts of me that ached from last night.

Lord Almighty. What the hell was I thinking going home with some stranger from a bar?

I should have known better. I shouldn't have let my anger about Ricky's no-good, cheating ass spur me on to do something stupid. Even if that led to the best night of my life.

That wasn't the point. The point was that I'd wasted four years of my life because some dreamer with a guitar sold me a line of bullshit I should have been able to smell from a thousand miles away. But I was too naive and trusting.

"Wait for me, Whitney. I'll move you down here as soon as I catch my big break."

Yeah. Right.

Ricky's voice was on every radio in the country while I was still in Gable, and apparently his dick was in every chick in LA.

My teenage dreams of being carried off into the sunset by my brother's best friend were officially shattered. *Ricky Rango, you can have your fame and your hos. What you will never have is Whitney Gable.*

After we'd had it out and I told him I was done, I'd gone to my closet and yanked out the first outfit that wouldn't make me feel like a cheated-on ex-girlfriend, and then went to the bar. I didn't even know if I was looking for a rebound. I'd just needed to feel *wanted.*

It was just my luck that I did find a rebound and had the best sex of my life. *And why did that rebound have to be Lincoln freaking Riscoff?*

"You missed a spot, Whit," Aunt Jackie called from behind me as she dusted the shelving units. "Top left corner. You know Rachelle will bitch if there's a single mark on her glass, and I'm not going to let her cheap ass dock my fee again."

As I reached up to get the spot Aunt Jackie pointed out, hazel eyes collided with mine through the window I was washing.

No. No. No. This wasn't happening. My stomach flip-flopped as Aunt Jackie's voice faded to static in my brain.

Only a single pane of glass with swirly silver letters separated me from Lincoln Riscoff. He stopped right in front of me, his eyebrows shooting up toward his dark brown hair.

Did he even recognize me? I looked nothing like I did last night. Now my long black hair was caught up in a red bandanna, and I was wearing cutoffs, old gym shoes, and a Bob Marley T-shirt.

When he lunged for the front door of the boutique, my

stomach dropped. He yanked on the door handle, but it didn't give.

Thank God it's locked.

"Open it." The glass wasn't thick enough to muffle his words completely.

I jerked my chin over my shoulder, but Aunt Jackie was gone—probably to empty the trash outside in the dumpster because we were almost done.

Thank the Lord. It was Sunday, so that meant I was using up my collateral with the Almighty pretty damn fast because it had been a long time since I'd been to church.

I shook my head and pointed to my ears and said the first thing I could think of. *"No hablo Español."*

His dark brows swooped together in a deep *V*, and I realized what just came out of my mouth. *What the hell is wrong with you, Whitney?*

His lips quirked as a smile spread over his face. "Open the door. I'm not done with you."

"I can't hear you."

He moved his face closer to the glass and said two words, enunciating carefully. "Bull. Shit."

I swallowed the lump in my throat, but the rest of my body froze in place. My tongue swept out over my dry-as-dust lips before I spoke. "I can't."

Lincoln glanced up at the sign above the door and gave me a chin jerk before turning and walking away. My entire body relaxed, and I spun around to slide down the glass until my butt hit the floor.

"Whit, I gotta make a phone call. Can't wait. Be back in ten. I'm locking you in," Aunt Jackie yelled from the back before the door shut and the bolt slid.

Thank you, Jackie.

I dropped my head into my hands and thought about the mess I'd just avoided.

Lincoln. Riscoff.

What was I thinking?

Oh, that's right. I wasn't thinking with my brain. Nope, just my neglected girl parts that got way too caught up in the moment when a guy stood up for me in a bar. I raised my head and whacked it against the glass to stare at the ceiling.

Dammit. I'm going to have to rewash this spot.

I was debating with myself about finding the will to stand again when the jangle of keys interrupted my self-ridiculing thoughts about what happened last night.

My head swiveled toward the door. He was back. With keys.

You have got to be kidding me. Clearly, my favors with God had run out.

The door swung open and a gust of wind hit me at the same time I realized I had zero protection from Lincoln Riscoff. He was inside.

My mouth moved but no words came out.

"My family owns this building. Property manager lives above the store at the end of the block. I ran."

My gaze locked on the hint of tanned throat and broad chest peeking out from his shirt collar, and my dumb ass couldn't stop wondering why he wasn't sweaty if he just ran. I was sweating like a pig and swearing like a trucker by the time I hit the main road this morning and flagged down Ginger Baskins on her way to church and told her my car broke down. Her side-eye was impressive and her disbelief apparent, but she gave me a ride home anyway—and told me I need Jesus.

I agree, Ginger. I agree.

Lincoln held out a hand to me. "We need to talk."

I stared at his capable fingers and neatly clipped nails like I'd never seen a hand before in my life. Let alone never let that hand do things to me that no man had ever done before. Things I liked. Way too much.

It was also the hand of the enemy.

"You won't even touch me now?"

I swallowed again and flicked my gaze up to his before looking back down at the floor I'd mopped an hour ago. "I'm dirty. You're . . ."

"A Riscoff. Which is why you ran this morning." His deep voice carried just a hint of roughness, and all I could think of was the thing that voice had said to me last night.

Because I'm an idiot.

"I shouldn't have left the bar with you."

"But you did. And you didn't have a single problem with it until you found out who I am. So, are you going to share with me what the hell made you run like you'd just discovered I had bodies hidden in the walls?"

My gaze darted up to his. "Do you?"

"What's your name, Blue?"

That nickname. It slayed me. I wished he hadn't said it, because now I wanted to tell him everything he wanted to know.

And . . . maybe telling him was the quickest way to get him to leave me alone.

I locked my stare with his, trying not to get lost in the green-and-gold depths, and told him. "Whitney Gable."

I was expecting shock—a comical level of it, to be honest —but instead I got no reaction from him at all. Maybe stonewalling emotions was something Riscoffs were required to master by age ten or something. Wouldn't surprise me since they were basically all spawned from the devil himself

—Commodore Riscoff. The man who burned down my family's homestead.

Instead of backing away like I was rabid, Lincoln moved his hand closer to me, and for some reason that, plus his continued silence, made me bolder.

"Did you not hear me? I'm a Gable. You're sworn to hate me for life. So, it would be better for both of us if you'd turn around and walk your privileged Riscoff ass out the door and let me get on with my day before my aunt gets back and sees you here."

Instead of doing what I told him, Lincoln squatted down until his face was only inches from mine. "I'm a Riscoff, which means I can do whatever the fuck I want, including not hating a Gable."

Shock filtered through me.

"At least now I get why you ran this morning. Gotta say, that was a first for me."

He reached down, bracketing my hips with both hands, and lifted me to my feet—and directly against his chest.

His heat soaked into my T-shirt that was micro thin from too many years of washing. My nipples hardened, and the jump of his Adam's apple told me he felt the hard points poking through the barely there fabric of my bra.

"I want to see you again." His breath brushed my ear as he leaned closer.

I wanted to push away to put space between us but couldn't bring myself to break his hold on me. "Didn't you hear what I said? I'm a Gable. Whatever you think is happening, it's not. You need to forget you've ever seen me. I can't—"

"Then tell me you don't want more, *Whitney Gable.* Tell me last night wasn't as good for you as it was for me."

His fingertips dug into my hips, and I wanted to rub up

against him like a cat in heat. Last night was incredible, and up until I saw the picture of Commodore Riscoff, Roosevelt Riscoff, and *him* and realized who he was, I was planning on having as many repeats as possible.

I forced myself to jerk out of his hold. "That doesn't matter. Your family stole our farm and burned it all down. You might not have been here for that, but we lost everything because of the Riscoffs."

I stalked across the floor, but he snagged my wrist and twirled me back around to face him.

"You're going to walk away because of some bullshit feud that should've been buried a hundred fucking years ago? Is that what you're seriously saying to me?"

"Yes! Maybe it's easy to dismiss it from up in the tower where you live, but—" I pointed to the bucket of water I'd been using to wash the windows. "Where I am, down on solid ground, we notice when someone takes something from us. We especially notice when they take everything."

His mouth twisted, and I thought I'd finally hammered home my point. I should have been thrilled as he dropped my wrist, but a sharp feeling stabbed me in the chest.

"Fuck that." Lincoln's deep voice turned harsh, and his expression went hard. "I don't give a damn. This isn't over between you and me."

He stepped forward and pulled me against him. My body responded with heat flaring between my legs, but my mind clanged like a warning bell.

I might as well have been deaf to it.

Lincoln's lips crashed against mine, kissing me like he was a dying man and I was his only hope of survival. I tried to keep my hands off him, but I failed miserably as I wrapped my arms around his neck to pull him closer.

Kissing Lincoln Riscoff was like finding salvation when

you'd thought all was lost. It didn't feel like kissing the enemy.

"What the hell is going on here?"

Aunt Jackie's voice cut through my rioting emotions, and I jerked back as Lincoln released me. I knew exactly when she recognized who he was by her sharp intake of breath.

"Holy shit, Whitney. Please tell me he's not who I think he is."

"Ma'am, I'm—"

I interrupted Lincoln before he could say any more. "He's leaving. Right now."

I could almost hear Lincoln's brain going to work as he opened his mouth to argue with me, but thankfully he listened to my request. He stepped away, and the next thing I heard was the tinkling chimes of the door as it opened and closed.

Aunt Jackie's furious gaze speared me. "You've got a hell of a lot of explaining to do, and I suggest you start right now."

LINCOLN

Present day

I SHAKE my head and hide a smile when Cricket Gable swings a U-turn on Bridge Street and narrowly misses cars and pedestrians. But that's until I see who's sitting in the passenger seat.

Fuck.

Her blue eyes are unforgettable. Ten years. Ten thousand years. It doesn't matter. I could never forget Whitney Gable's blue eyes. I've been bullshitting myself for a decade if I thought I could.

Everything comes rushing back like a tornado twisting through my body and into my blood, until I swear she's under my skin again already.

Who the fuck am I kidding? She's always been under my skin. I've spent a decade trying to forget, and I was lying to myself if I thought I'd made a damn bit of progress.

Whitney Gable isn't a woman you forget. She's a woman you kill to keep.

And I failed at that.

I haven't failed at anything since then—except marrying a woman and producing the heir Commodore has been demanding. I still don't know how the old man knew she was coming back, but I've spent all day telling myself it didn't matter.

More lies to myself.

She'll always fucking matter.

You never forget the girl who shattered your heart and left you a different man than you were before you met her. You never forget how you strapped on armor over the holes she left after you publicly humiliated yourself for her.

And I would do it again if there was a chance I could have stopped her from marrying Ricky Rango.

But he's dead now, and Whitney's fair game. She's only gotten better with age. Instead of the beautiful girl she was then, now she's a devastating woman . . .

I squint for a better look because something dark mars the side of her face and below her eye. Does she have a black eye?

A rush of anger hits my bloodstream when I see the undeniable bruising, even as she fumbles to slip on giant sunglasses like she's always wearing in the photos that hit the tabloids even I can't avoid.

Who the fuck touched her? If Ricky Rango were still alive, I'd put him in the ground, even though he's been dead too long to have given her a black eye.

I stare at her through the windshield. *Ricky Rango's Black Widow.*

Can someone really change that much?

Part of me wants to say yes, she's savage enough to kill a man, because it nearly killed me when she left ten years ago, but that's the bitter side of me. The man she rejected all too publicly.

The rest of me . . . I don't think it's possible.

"Hey, baby!" Cricket yells from the window she's climbed completely out of rather than opening the door.

Hunter walks around her piece-of-shit van to talk to his fiancée, leaving me standing on the sidewalk, staring at Whitney Gable through glass.

Just like it did all those years ago, my mouth grows a mind of its own, completely separate from my brain.

"Open it."

Whitney keeps her eyes focused straight ahead and pretends she doesn't hear me.

We both know she's full of shit, and not just because the muscles of her throat work as she swallows. She made me believe she wanted nothing from me. Made me believe I was nothing to her. From the pulse hammering under the smooth skin of her neck, I know she fucking lied.

I step closer.

"Open the window, Whitney." Her name hasn't come out of my mouth in ten years, but goddamn, does it feel good on my lips. "You know you're going to have to face me eventually."

Her lips press together into a flat line while she continues to ignore me.

Cricket and Hunter's conversation may as well be happening on another planet, because the only two people that exist in this world are me and the woman who wants to pretend I don't.

"Listen up, Blue. You're back in my town. My world. You can hear me. You can see me. You can pretend I'm not here all you want, but I am." I rest an elbow on the window and lean closer. "And there's one other thing you should know. *We aren't fucking done.*"

Her shoulders tense and her chin jerks in my direction.

49

Finally, a reaction.

I wish I could rip those sunglasses off her face and see her eyes again, but I'll settle for this . . . for now.

"I'll be seeing you soon, Blue. Really soon."

Whitney's bottom lip drops and quivers, and more than anything, I want to close my teeth around it and remind her how much she fucking loved to kiss me.

My body remembers. It comes to life, my heart pumping faster, my fingers itching to touch her.

The driver door shuts after Cricket climbs back inside, and I step back.

"This isn't over, Whitney Gable. Not by a long shot."

With a calculating smile, I shove my hands in my pockets and turn away from the van as Cricket guns it, spinning tires as she pulls away from the sidewalk. Hunter and I both stare after it and I try to act casual, even though Whitney Gable bursting back into my life again is anything but.

"You need to give your girl driving lessons, Hunt," I say, watching the van head down the road.

Hunter's laugh rings out. "Nah, I like her just the way she is. Fucking crazy. Might get her a safer car, though."

I shoot a look at my best friend. "A tank?"

He grins. "Not a bad idea. I'll look into it." He glances at the taillights and then back to me. "Will you and Cricket's cousin be able to make it through our wedding without killing each other?"

A smile tugs at the corners of my mouth.

"Killing Whitney Gable is the last thing I want to do."

WHITNEY

"Are you still hungry? Because you look like you're about to puke," Cricket says, drawing my attention away from the dash that's covered in stickers, mostly of pot leaves and unicorns.

Puke? Maybe.

Run screaming out of Gable because Lincoln Riscoff scares the ever-loving hell out of me? Definitely.

But that's not something I want to admit to my cousin out loud.

"Umm," I mumble because I truly don't know what to say to her. I hate that he got to me so quickly. I hate that he still affects me like that. I also hate that I heard every single word he said, and that bastard knew it.

"Because if you're not going to puke, guac and queso make everything better." She scans my face and apparently finds the answers she's looking for. "I think you're still up for Cocko Taco. But all you have to do is say the word, and I'll promise to hit Lincoln Riscoff if I see him on the sidewalk again, instead of letting him try to talk to you."

I whip my head sideways. "You acted like you didn't even notice he was there."

Cricket's crooked grin and dancing eyes give her away.

"You did it on purpose? You whore! You're my cousin. My best friend! How could you do that to me?"

She bites her lip and shrugs as she pulls into Cocko Taco and parks beneath the sign and next to the giant rooster made of red, blue, and yellow metal welded together like yard art.

"Cricket . . ."

She turns toward me as my unspoken threat trails off.

"You had to face him sometime. When I saw them on the sidewalk, I thought it would be like ripping off a Band-Aid. Now it's over and done with, and you don't have to spend time worrying about him anymore. Your anxiety was messing with your energy. You've been a hot mess ever since you got in the van. I could feel it rolling off you. I'm trying to help you find some Zen, Whit."

I cover my face with both hands and drop my head back against the headrest. "I know what you're trying to do, but I was perfectly content with my plan to avoid him for the rest of my natural life. It was a great plan. Fucking amazing."

"It was a terrible plan."

"And why's that?" I peek through my fingers to see my cousin looking at me like I'm an idiot.

"The wedding? We have a bunch of wedding festivities planned, and he'll be there. Plus . . . Hunter's mom insisted it all be at The Gables."

My fingers snap closed and I stop looking at my cousin because I don't want her to see my look of horror.

The Gables. Great. Only one of the fanciest mountainside resorts in the world, and *owned by the Riscoffs.*

"Are you sure you don't want Karma to be your maid of honor?" I ask the windshield.

Cricket lays a hand on my arm. "No, Whit. I want you. If you truly can't handle it, I'll understand. But . . . I will hold it against you forever."

"Whore," I mumble under my breath.

"No, that's Karma. I've got zero kids, and she has *two* with no baby-daddy in sight."

I draw in a deep breath and try to find the strength to tell my cousin it's fine. I can do this. I won't flake out on her like I basically have for the last ten years.

"I'm picking out my own dress, and I get to throw you whatever kind of bachelorette party I want."

Her squeal fills the van. "Fuck yes!" She lunges across the center console and wraps her arms around me. "Thank you, Whit. You're the best, and I love you so much. It'll be great. I promise. You won't even notice he exists."

And that's where Cricket is dead wrong. Pretending Lincoln Riscoff doesn't exist is impossible.

I already tried it once, and I remember exactly how that turned out . . .

WHITNEY

The past

"I'VE GOT something you might want."

His voice.

My head jerked up and I looked around, thinking I must have been hallucinating, but no. I wasn't.

Lincoln Riscoff was standing in the doorway of the Havalins' bathroom, holding my abandoned boot, while I was on my hands and knees scrubbing grout.

Awesome. Why don't we just take a scene right out of Cinderella? The prince bringing around a shoe to fit the maid.

I tore my gaze away from my favorite boot dangling in front of my face and forced my attention back to the grout.

I will not acknowledge him. I will not give him the satisfaction.

I also wouldn't think about how my lips tingled when I remembered what it felt like to kiss him.

"Whitney—"

"Go away." I bit out the words as humiliation burned my

skin. I wasn't ashamed of cleaning. It was honest work, and I needed all the money I could save if I was ever going to get out of this town. But I hated having him standing over me like he was better than me.

"Give me a goddamned chance, Blue. You did when you didn't know my name."

"I'm working. Leave me alone." I scrubbed harder, digging the toothbrush between the edges of the expensive tile.

"Just look at me. I'm not giving up. I'll stand here all day, if that's what it takes."

My lips screwed together in an angry moue and I bolted to my feet, one hand on my hip and the other jabbing the toothbrush into his chest.

"You can stand wherever you want. That's what Riscoffs do, right? Whatever the hell they want. Guess what? Not everyone has that privilege. Some of us have work to do, and you're in my way."

Something flashed across his hazel gaze, and it softened.

"I can't stop thinking about you." His roughened words sounded completely honest.

It was such a simple thing to say, but it was beyond effective. When was the last time someone *thought* about me? I'd always been the afterthought.

I squeezed my eyes shut. It would be so easy to fall under Lincoln's spell, especially because I hadn't been able to stop thinking about him or how he made me feel.

Until I found out his name.

"Why can't you be someone else," I whispered, wanting to take the words back as soon as they escaped my lips.

When his hand closed over mine, the toothbrush fell to the tile, and the boot landed beside it.

"Why can't you see me the way you did before you knew who I was?"

I looked away, down toward the corner of the room. "It's not that easy. You don't understand. You won. We lost."

Lincoln's fingers curved under my chin and redirected my gaze to his. "I wouldn't say I'm winning right now. I'm looking at the only thing I want, and you're telling me it's impossible because of our last names. I don't buy that. I will *never* buy that. Just give me a goddamned chance. That's all you have to do."

"Whitney? You done up there yet?"

My aunt's voice cut between us more effectively than a freshly sharpened ax. She was downstairs cleaning with my mom and cousin. After Jackie saw us together last time, she spared me the lecture, but her harsh stare said more than enough. Basically, *what the hell are you thinking?* If my mom were to come up . . .

"I need ten more minutes!"

"And I need ten more years," Lincoln said, his voice rougher as it turned deeper and more desperate. "Maybe that would be enough to get you out of my system, but I doubt it."

His words hit me hard and my blood heated. I wanted him more than I'd ever wanted anyone.

"We can't do this. If my family found out . . . they'd disown me."

"No one has to know but us. Not until we want them to know."

"They could *never* know."

Victory flashed in his gaze, making me want to snatch back the words, because it sounded like I'd made a decision.

Have I?

As soon as his knuckles brushed along the skin of my bicep, my entire body trembled, telling me I had decided.

I was going to go against everything I'd been taught my entire life—that Riscoffs were evil, money-grubbing, dishonest, no-good cheats—and I was going to have an affair with the heir to the empire.

"Meet me tonight at the cabin. Eleven o'clock."

He pulled me against him, and as soon as his lips hit mine, I knew this was the only choice I could have made. I couldn't walk away from this yet. I needed more of how he made me feel. *Like I matter.*

It was intoxicating.

I just didn't realize addiction was the first step toward my downfall.

"I'll be there."

LINCOLN

Present day

FROM THE WINDOWS of my office, I stare down the river as it runs fast through the gorge with the runoff from the mountain snow melt. Massive trees block my view of much else. It's those massive trees that created my family's legacy after the Gables jumped the claim to our gold mine in 1851.

That didn't work out so well for the Gables, though, because the mine petered out long before they learned to make good business decisions or save a dime. My forefathers left fools' dreams of gold behind and went to the woods, building the country's largest timber company and lodging themselves firmly into history as lumber barons. Or as some called them after they added railroads to family business—robber barons.

Riscoff Holdings still takes a top spot on the list of largest privately held companies in the country. But it's not just a company; it's a family dynasty. This town may bear the Gable name, but we own damn near every inch of it. Nothing happens in Gable that we don't have a hand in.

I have to wonder if that includes Whitney Gable's return, especially since Commodore knew she was coming.

Now I need to decide how I'm going to handle it. I've seen her. I want her.

If she were anyone else, she'd be in my bed tonight. Women hear the Riscoff name and see dollar signs instead of a man. Whitney Gable is the only woman who has had the exact opposite reaction, and that's only one piece of what set her apart from all the rest.

My need to see her again drives me just as hard as the knowledge that I should stay away. I already publicly humiliated myself once for her, and that's not an experience I'm eager to repeat.

Then again, maybe I shouldn't have objected at her wedding.

But she didn't love Ricky Rango. She couldn't have. I didn't believe it then, and I don't believe it now. Not after those months she spent with me.

Could I have handled it better? Absolutely. I should have skipped the two fifths of Scotch before I walked into that church. Even though I was drunk, I still remember what she said to me that day. *"You can't buy me."*

I've spent a decade waiting for my second chance. Now that it's here, I'm not going to fuck it up again. If this were a business deal, I'd identify weaknesses, exploit them, and win. I should apply the same strategy to Whitney.

Should.

But for some goddamned reason, I want her to come to me of her own free will—totally and completely.

I won't settle for scraps this time. I don't want stolen nights and hidden meetings. I want her out in the open. In front of God and the entire world.

And that will never happen with Whitney.

Bullshit. I refuse to believe it. I've worked myself to the bone over the last decade, punishing myself for my stupidity and obsession as I added million after million to the Riscoff bank accounts.

I deserve a damn reward, and that reward is Whitney Gable.

And if I can't get her on my own terms? Then what?

It's no longer a case of being able to buy and sell the Gables. They've faltered as we've risen.

We *own* them.

We own damn near everyone. Eighty percent of the residents of Gable work for the Riscoff family, whether it's in timber, railroad, the mill, the bank, or other business holdings. We built the hospitals, the schools, the parks, the new bus terminal, the community center, and the regional airport. We loan money to businesses to keep the local economy growing, and sponsor art exhibits to expose the residents to culture.

This city may not bear our name, yet it's ours all the same.

But Whitney Gable's words are still burned into my brain.

"You can't buy me."

I hope it doesn't come to the point where I find out she was lying. I want to believe she's still different from everyone else.

WHITNEY

THIS AFTERNOON HAS BEEN a trip down memory lane, and I've hit every pothole in the road. I wanted to sneak back into Gable quietly, without anyone being the wiser, hug my cousin and my aunt and lick my wounds in peace for a while. Clearly, that wasn't in the cards.

After stuffing ourselves at Cocko Taco, I'm feeling a tiny bit better about my decision to return. Top-notch guac and queso can do that for a girl.

Cricket guides her van down roads I know by heart, but they look different after ten years away. Older houses that were beyond repair have been replaced with new construction. The high school looks like it's brand new, and the Riscoff Memorial High sign out front reminds me of the man I just saw.

Before today, it was easier not to think about all the things that have been changing in my absence. Including the fact that Lincoln has aged better than the Italian wine Ricky once tried to collect but drank within months instead . . . right before his first stint in rehab.

Cricket turns left down Aunt Jackie's street, and I catch a

glimpse of the mountain peaks rising above the tall pines. At least some things don't change.

"Beware, Karma's been in the shittiest mood for the last couple months, and I have no idea why. I think she's pregnant again, but I'm afraid to ask her. Lord knows, the last time I asked that, she ripped me a new one."

"Again?"

Cricket nods.

"Is she still seeing the twins' dad?"

"Lord only knows. She won't tell me anything. It's like the older she gets, the bitchier she gets, which means there's pretty much no end in sight to this downward spiral."

When we were growing up, I always had Asa, and he'd taken his role as big brother seriously, scaring off any guy who looked my way. Other than that, as far as siblings went, he was a pretty damn good one overall. I've been saved from ever wanting a sister, though, because of Karma.

I brace for impact as we roll into the driveway and Cricket shifts the van into park. The front door swings open as she and I grab my bags out of the back and carry them to the front stoop.

"Knew you'd come crawling home eventually, and here you are."

Karma's voice should sound exactly like Cricket's, but years of bitterness, starting when she was a kid and wanted a pony but Jackie couldn't afford one, have turned it hard and mean. She leans against the door, not moving out of the way, even though it's clear we're headed inside.

I stop before the stairs and release the handle of one suitcase. "Hey, Karma. It's good to see you."

Her lip curls. "You look like LA chewed you up and kicked you to the curb." Her gaze drops to my suitcase. "But you managed to make it out with your fancy luggage, didn't you?"

"Really? That's how you're going to say hello after ten freaking years? You're a cunt." Cricket holds nothing back when it comes to her twin.

Karma's tawny gaze shifts to her sister as she glares. "Takes one to know one. You're just all high-and-mighty because you're locking down Hunter Havalin's dick. I guess I should've taken him for a ride when I had the chance."

I step back like I'm trying to escape the cloud of venom she emits. It should be impossible for two people who look exactly alike to be so completely different.

"I'm not sure what planet you're living on, but you never had a chance with Hunter. He knew you were a ho from minute one. Now, why don't you swallow back that bitterness and get out of the damn way so we can take Whitney's stuff inside."

"And where exactly is she going to sleep? If you don't recall, you're sleeping on the couch when you're here, because we don't have any more room."

"Maybe if you'd keep your legs closed, we wouldn't have that problem," Cricket fires back with a hard shot.

"Bitch."

"Whore."

I step in because I'm afraid there's going to be bloodshed if I don't. There certainly was in the past. "Okay, enough of the sisterly bonding. I'll take the floor in the living room. It's not a big deal. I just need somewhere to crash while I figure things out. If that's not cool with Aunt Jackie, I'll get a cheap hotel." I don't have the funds to afford it, but right now, I'm not sure I want to be in the same house with Karma and her ugliness.

"There's a shed out back with a futon Mom used to use

for her art projects. There should be room for you and your shit." Karma shoves a toe against my carry-on and knocks it over.

I bite my tongue because it's not going to do me any good to be outraged. It's just luggage. I didn't even want the stuff, but Ricky got so focused on appearances, he wouldn't hear of his wife showing up with American Tourister and embarrassing him.

"Fine. I'll take the shed. At least it's getting warm."

Karma crosses her arms.

"Don't you have to go get the girls?"

Karma's glare swings to her sister. "Don't tell me how to raise my kids."

"Whatever. Just get out of our way if you're not going to help."

"Done." Karma turns her back, slips into the house, and lets the door slam in our faces.

"Jesus Christ, I didn't realize there was any way she could have possibly gotten worse, but . . . wow."

Cricket shakes her head. "I told you, it's been awful lately. I swear, she needs a joint and a good fuck—with a condom, so she doesn't get knocked up again. Maybe she'd be in a better mood if Addy or Maddy's daddy, whoever he might be, would show any interest in their kids."

"I guess that's enough to make anyone bitter."

A pang of sympathy for Karma's kids stabs me in the chest. It reminds me of my childhood, which was nowhere near perfect either. But instead of being angry all the time, my mom was a ghost and my dad was always pissed off and looking for her. He didn't hesitate to take it out on me with the back of his hand when I got too old for his belt.

"Mom and I try to make up for it. Some days, Karma

doesn't even get out of bed, so we don't have much choice in the matter."

I think about what Cricket said her sister needed. "Sounds like she needs medication and a major attitude adjustment."

"Something. She's damn near unbearable. I try to avoid her as much as possible. I sleep on the couch or crash with Hunter. Hell, some nights I even sleep in my van because being around her is too much to take." Cricket pauses. "Honestly, the shed really isn't a bad idea. Mom fixed the place up during her DIY phase. Let's go check it out and see if we can't make it work."

With a bag in each of our hands, Cricket and I head through the house, which has been updated since I left. The striped wallpaper in the hallway is gone, replaced by bright yellow paint. The couch in the living room is red leather now instead of tan cloth that I remember. The kitchen cabinets have been painted white and sanded in the corners for an artfully worn effect, and the countertops look new.

Cricket opens the back door and leads me out into the yard. The grass is neatly mowed and lilacs line the fence. Aunt Jackie hasn't done too bad for herself, which is at least one more thing to be happy about today.

In the far corner, near the back gate, is a wooden shed hiding behind raised beds holding vine-covered lattice.

"I haven't been back here in ages," Cricket says as we cross the lawn. "I don't think Mom has used it in a while either. She gave up on painting and has gotten more into gardening with the girls."

I open the door and peek inside, shocked to see that it's not stuffed with old junk, but is instead a cute little living area with a futon. I flip on the light switch and smile at the shabby-chic interior. The table and two chairs, futon, coffee table, and rugs are no doubt from yard sales, but that doesn't take away from their charm. The curtains are lacy and, if I had to guess, sewn by my aunt's own hand.

It's a she-shed.

A stack of outdated magazines and a few shelves of dusty books and an easel prove this is definitely Aunt Jackie's haven from the world. Part of me feels guilty about intruding, but if there's not room in the house for me, I don't think she'll mind, especially since the layer of dust on everything says she hasn't used it in a while.

Growing up, I spent as much time with Jackie and Cricket as I could rather than with my own family. They lived in a house down by the river, only a quarter mile from my folks' place on the family farm that went up for auction . . . before Commodore Riscoff burned it down. After the sheriff threw us out, we were all scrambling for someplace to live, and Jackie landed here with the girls. My dad rented us a little place on the wrong side of the tracks that was barely big enough for three people.

"It's perfect," I say to Cricket as she sets one of my bags down just inside.

"It's actually nicer than I remember. I should've moved out here. I don't know why I didn't think of it. I totally forgot Mom put plumbing in herself, so there's even a bathroom."

Instantly, I feel bad. "Do you want it? I can find something else."

"No. I'm moving in with Hunter after the wedding, and I don't mind couch surfing in the meantime."

"Not that it's any of my business, but . . . why haven't you already moved in with him?"

Cricket shrugs before plopping down on the futon, and I sit next to her. "His mom made it clear that she'd be completely scandalized if I move in any sooner."

The tone of her voice alerts me to trouble.

"You and Mrs. Havalin don't get along?"

"Honestly?"

"Well, yeah."

"She didn't want Hunter ending up with a Gable."

I wince because I'm sure my reputation around town didn't help with that. "She actually told you that?"

Cricket tilts her head from side to side. "Not in so many words, but she's made it clear that any other family wouldn't leave her footing the whole bill for the wedding."

"I shouldn't say this, but I already don't like your mother-in-law to be."

"It can always be worse, right?"

I wonder if she's thinking of Mrs. Riscoff, because Lincoln's mother would be the mother-in-law from hell. *Why am I even thinking about him, let alone his mother?* I force the image of Mrs. Riscoff's face, pinched in disapproval, from my memory.

"What does Hunter say about it?"

The glowing smile that takes over Cricket's face is something so pure, I wish I could snap a picture without her noticing. *She loves him. Really loves him.*

"He doesn't give a damn. We actually were going to elope until his dad made a big speech about his son getting married in Gable, surrounded by all his friends and family." Cricket's glow fades. "So . . . I told him we should do it if it mattered to them."

"Are you sure that's what you really want?" I hate the thought of my free-spirited cousin feeling like a guest at her own wedding.

"Hunter would tell them all to fuck off if I told him I didn't want to do it. But I know that his dad doesn't have a lot of years left, and I actually like the old man, so I'm not going to make waves."

She drags her finger through the layer of dust on the magazines stacked on the coffee table. "Although, with it being at The Gables, Mrs. Havalin will probably have kittens and want to invite everyone in the known universe to show off that they're close to the Riscoffs. But . . . at least it takes the pressure off me, right? Who will even bother to look at the bride when the heir to a billion-dollar company is standing in the front row."

I brush Cricket's brown hair away from her face so I can see her eyes. "Hey. Stop that. It's your big day. Fuck Lincoln Riscoff."

Cricket's lips quirk. "Sorry, Whit. You already did. I don't like sloppy seconds."

WHITNEY

The past

MY BODY WAS BUZZING when I reached the cabin.

I shouldn't be here. I knew that as plainly as I knew I shouldn't gargle Drano or play with gasoline and matches in a barn filled with hay, but I couldn't stop myself.

Although I reached out to knock, my knuckles never connected with the door. Lincoln whipped it open, his chest rising and falling, before I could make contact.

"I didn't think you were going to come. I thought I'd have to hunt you down again."

Lord, he's way too attractive for his own good.

His hazel eyes raked up and down my body as I stared at the pulse thumping at the base of his throat, trying to talk myself out of licking his skin to remind myself what he tasted like.

Oh my God, Whitney, what the hell is wrong with you?

Lincoln Riscoff. He was what was wrong with me. I hadn't been able to get him off my mind since the other night.

It was like I was broken, and only another night with him could fix it.

"I wasn't going to come. I talked myself out of it at least a hundred times."

His nostrils flared.

That should not be sexy.

"What made you change your mind?"

"Do you want the truth?" My voice sounded husky and not at all like me.

He nodded.

I swallowed and decided if I was going to do this . . . I was going to *do it*.

"This." I launched myself at him, not even caring that it made me look just like the kind of girl I claimed not to be the other night. But Lincoln didn't seem to mind one bit.

He braced and caught me, his hands curving around the cheeks of my ass in my cut-off shorts, and pulled me against him. I didn't dress fancy tonight. Not like I did when I went to the bar. I came as basic as I usually am . . . cutoffs, flip-flops, T-shirt, my hair in a wild cloud around my head.

"Thank fuck," he growled as our mouths collided.

I wrapped my fingers around the back of his neck and took control of the kiss, pushing my tongue between his lips. I knew all too well that this was crazy, but the urgency I felt was impossible to ignore. Something about this man made me forget all my better judgment because I just needed *him*.

"I would've come for you," he said against my mouth.

In my head, I thought, *oh, you're going to come for me, all right*, but I was too caught up in tasting him to pull away and actually say it.

My fingers moved from his neck to the material of his T-shirt, and I bunched it in my fingers, pulling it up his back. I wanted to see him again. Wanted to feel him again.

He carried me back to the bedroom and lowered me to the bed. I held on to the fabric, tugging the shirt over his head as he rose.

His chest, shoulders, and arms looked like he should be on the cover of a magazine. Those celebrity guys I used to drool over on TV? They didn't even look like this. And don't get me started on his abs. I didn't know that was a real thing. Like a freaking washboard I could use for laundry. It took me longer than I planned to drag my attention back to his face, because my gaze snagged on the bulge in his jeans.

His hazel eyes burned bright with desire. "You're killing me, Blue. Fucking killing me."

"I want you." It was the truth, plain and simple.

"Not half as bad as I want you."

"I don't know about that," I said, my gaze dipping back to his cock. Last time we were here, Lincoln went down on me —a first I'd never forget—and tonight, I wanted to return the favor. Maybe I was hoping then he'd feel as out of control as I did. Whatever the reason, the idea turned into a compulsion.

I reached for the button of his jeans, and his hazel eyes locked on my hands.

"You don't have to—"

"Shut up. Unless you want me to lose my nerve."

His hands covered mine. "Whitney—"

I glanced up as his tone softened. "Blue. You call me Blue."

His lips pressed together and he gave me a nod, and I released his zipper before sliding my hand into his jeans. I closed my fingers around his cock, and he sucked in a hissing breath.

"Jesus fucking Christ. How do your hands feel so damn good?"

"I don't know, but I guarantee my mouth is going to feel

even better."

I levered up further on the bed and guided him toward me so he was standing between my knees. Then I leaned over and swiped at the head of his cock with my tongue.

Another sharp indrawn breath told me he was a fan. I grew bolder and sucked the head into my mouth.

His fingers tangled in my hair. "Goddammit, woman. You're going to kill me."

I pulled back and looked up between my lashes, feeling a heady rush of power. "Try not to die before you carry through on your promise."

He opened his mouth to speak, but I closed my lips over the head again and sucked. I'd never felt such an intense need to bring a man to his knees, but with this man, everything was different.

Maybe it was because I was a Gable and he was a Riscoff. That my very presence here was completely in the realm of the forbidden. Whatever it was that was driving me, skills I never knew I possessed come to the forefront, and I worked him over so well that I was confident he'd never forget me.

Before I could finish him off, he grasped the sides of my head gently and pulled free of my mouth. I glanced up again, and his chest was heaving even harder than when he met me at the door.

"Why did—"

"I'm not coming in your mouth. Not when I know how sweet your pussy is."

Good Lord. I didn't know if was the intensity of his stare or his dirty words, but another rush of heat surged between my legs.

"Then what are you waiting for?" I fell back on my elbows on the bed.

Lincoln's teeth dragged over his lower lip, and I could tell he wanted to eat me alive.

"Fuck, you do something to me, Blue. I gotta have you. Now." He reached forward and dragged my shorts down my legs before tossing them to the floor. "This is gonna get a little rough. Speak now or . . ."

I knew what he meant. I knew what he felt. I met his gaze, matching his intensity with every heartbeat."

"Don't hold back."

He kicked out of his jeans and grabbed them to retrieve a condom from the pocket. As soon as he rolled it on, he pressed both palms to the bed, bracketing my hips.

"Sorry about your panties."

I opened my mouth to ask what he meant, but he slid a finger under the lace and tugged before I could form words. The elastic snapped.

Holy hell, that was hot.

When Lincoln moved between my thighs, I'd never been more turned on in my life. I thought I was imagining how incredible we were together that night, but I didn't.

It wasn't the tequila or the rebound. It was him.

"Jesus Christ, you feel even better than I remember. How is that even possible?"

I didn't say it out loud, but I knew it was a simple fact that when you mixed Lincoln Riscoff and me together, we exploded like TNT.

Even though I knew it would blow up in our faces, I couldn't stop.

I let my head fall back and stopped worrying about the consequences, losing myself to his deliciously rough rhythm. My fingers clawed at the quilt as he pounded into me and took me all the way to the edge.

When I came, it was with the name of the enemy on my lips.

LINCOLN

Present day

"HEARD your old whore is back in town. Maybe she wants to take a younger Riscoff for a ride this time," Harrison says as he walks in late for our meeting.

I look up from the papers on the desk in front of me, the urge to kill my brother roaring to life with just a shred less ferocity as the urge to fire him.

If it weren't for Commodore's restriction on me removing my brother from employment without cause, his ass would be out of this company in a heartbeat. There is no love lost between me and my brother. Not after he fucked the woman I almost married just to prove he could. He did save me from an expensive divorce, though, so maybe I should thank him for that.

But I won't.

I stay seated and rein in my temper. I know what he wants —to bait me into slamming my fist into his face so he can go crying to Commodore and show him I'm unfit to inherit the Riscoff family holdings. There's no way in hell I'll give him the satisfaction. Instead, I direct my gaze to the clock on my desk.

"You're late. Your report is late."

His lips flatten into a frustrated line as he tosses a bound stack of paper onto my desk. "It's not late enough to matter."

If I were born the second son, and therefore wouldn't inherit anything because of an antiquated family tradition, I'd probably hate my older brother too. However, after a lifetime of dealing with his bullshit, there's no way in hell I would voluntarily step aside to let him run this company.

He drops into one of the chairs in front of my desk. "So, big brother, have you seen her yet? Or has she been rode hard and put up wet for too many years to catch your eye again?"

My fists clench again, and there's nothing more I'd like to do than grab him by the throat and hang him out the window until he screams like a bitch. Instead, I use what feels like superhuman control to grab the report and flip open to the executive summary on three acquisitions we're considering.

Thankfully, he keeps his mouth shut while I review it.

My gaze sharpens on his conclusion that we should enter the auction process for Tordon Industries. It has the best numbers of the three and would give us the best platform to leverage our strengths into the services industry. Diversification is vital at this point in our life cycle. We have to evolve and continue to grow beyond the current holdings if we want to remain relevant in today's economy. But just because Harrison isn't fucking up the big picture doesn't mean he's not burying something else in this report that could torpedo the acquisition. Which means I'll have to scour every page with a fine-tooth comb to make sure there's not something I'm missing.

Having a vice president with ulterior motives is fucking exhausting, because it means I'm doing both his job and mine to make sure he can't intentionally or unintentionally fuck the company over. He's the only person who would dare defy me in my role as CEO, but having my hands tied by Commodore as chairman of the board forces me to be extra vigilant. There's no time to turn my back on him for a second.

"So, have you seen her?" Of course Harrison won't fucking let it go.

"Can we get back to business?"

My brother kicks back in the chair, balancing it on the rear two legs.

One tip. That's all it would take to send him over.

I resist. Barely.

"She is business, as far as I'm concerned. You lost your fucking mind over her years ago, and I need to know, as vice president of this company, if I need to worry about you pulling a repeat performance."

I level a stare on my brother that would have any other man scuttling out of my presence, mumbling apologies as he went. Harrison's lip just curls.

"I'm not having this conversation with you."

He ignores my warning tone and keeps pushing. "I wonder how Mother will handle Whitney Gable coming back?"

My jaw clenches and I grit my teeth together as I count to ten. "Clearly, you don't have enough fucking work if you've got all this time to spend on gossip." I reach into the drawer of my desk and pull out a thick file. "We have a litigation matter I'd like you to assist legal with. It's a property dispute that we've been dealing with for ten years and haven't been able to resolve. I'm sure you can handle it."

Harrison's eyes narrow. "I don't want to deal with that shit."

"Good thing it's my decision and not yours." I let go of

my copy of the old file and it lands between us with a thump. "You're excused. If I find any errors in your report, I'll let you know."

My brother picks up the file.

"You think you're so high-and-mighty, big brother? You know what they say—the bigger they are . . ." He smirks and laughs. "I'm going to find some popcorn and get ready for the explosion that comes when Mother finds out Whitney Gable didn't stay gone. I hope your whore showing back up doesn't put her heart over the edge."

WHITNEY

Aunt Jackie's voice booms through the backyard.

"Lord Almighty! Someone tell me I'm hallucinating, because I can't believe what I'm seeing with my own eyes. My Whitney is home! Girl, get over here and give me a hug. It's been too damn long since I've seen your beautiful face."

Tears prick behind my eyes at the sight of her with outstretched arms. Unlike Karma, Aunt Jackie is beyond happy to see me.

I step toward her, letting the shed's screen slap shut behind me. As soon as she envelops me in a hug, a wave of belonging washes over me. She rocks me from side to side.

"Sweet girl, we missed you. It's been too damn long since you set foot in this town. Coming down to see you in LA wasn't the same. You weren't yourself there."

"I know. I'm sorry. I should've—"

"Shhh. I shouldn't be giving you hell for getting out of here and living. I sure can't fault you for that. I'm just happy you've finally found your way home again. Welcome back."

Now I wish I'd come home sooner, and maybe for reasons other than the fact that I have no place else to go.

"I thought you had to work until six? Are you going to get in trouble for leaving early?" Cricket asks as Jackie releases me, and I dash away a stray tear.

Jackie shakes her head. "Of course not. I'm the boss. Unless my job isn't being done satisfactorily, no one will fuss."

My eyes widen. "The boss?"

"Head of housekeeping at The Gables."

I blink a few times. "I can't believe they'd let a Gable work there, let alone be in charge."

Jackie smiles proudly. "Ms. Riscoff doesn't share the same prejudices as the rest of her family, and since she's CEO of the resort, working there is pretty damn fine."

I didn't think my eyes could get any wider, but I would have been wrong. "Little McKinley Riscoff is CEO of The Gables?"

I can't picture Lincoln's younger and painfully shy sister being in charge of anything, let alone an entire resort. His douchebag younger brother, Harrison? Sure. But McKinley seemed determined to blend into the background wherever she went.

"She's a fair boss and runs a tight ship. You won't hear me say a word against her." Jackie pauses. "She's not like the rest of them. She's good people."

I'm going to have to take Jackie's word for it because I don't plan on finding out myself.

"So, tell me everything. How are you? You okay? The tabloids have been vicious, but you know we don't believe a goddamned thing they say."

I drop my gaze to the ground. It's harder to lie to Jackie when I'm looking her in the eye. "I'm okay. I'm going to be okay."

My aunt's rough finger slides under my chin, and she tilts

my head up. She surveys my face, touching my cheekbone lightly with her other thumb. "Looks like you didn't duck quick enough. What the hell happened?"

Her question tugs a hint of a smile from my lips. "Angry fan. There have been a lot of those lately. I'm just hoping they don't follow me here."

She squares her shoulders. "Don't you worry about that. We shoot first and ask questions later. If I don't recognize someone, they're trespassing, and I don't miss."

That wave of warmth envelops me again. "Thank you. I really didn't want to bring my mess to your doorstep, but . . ."

Jackie hugs me again before pulling back to glance between Cricket and me. "Thank *you* for coming back. Cricket won't tell you, but this wedding business is running her ragged. I'm worried Mrs. Havalin is going to steamroll my girl."

"Mom—" Cricket protests.

"It's the truth, and you know it." Jackie's tone invites no argument. "You need backup because you won't say a damn thing you think around that woman, and Whitney will help you find your backbone."

Guilt for not coming home sooner overwhelms me. "I'm so sorry. I wish I'd known sooner. I'll do whatever I can to help."

Cricket glares at her mom. "I'm not a doormat. I'll speak up when it matters. Some things are just easier if I don't rock the boat." She cuts her gaze to me. "Besides, Whitney was fighting her own battles."

I can almost feel them both staring at my black eye when Jackie steps between us and squeezes both Cricket and me against her. "My sweet girls. I just want the best for both of you. That's all I've ever wanted. Now we're all here, and Gables are stronger together."

Gables are stronger together. I'm not sure I've ever thought of myself as *strong,* but if that's what Cricket needs me to be, I'll do it. *Which includes steering clear of Lincoln Riscoff.*

Resolve fills me. I finally feel like I have a purpose that goes beyond hiding from the press and fading into obscurity, and that purpose helps me straighten my shoulders.

I give Aunt Jackie a one-armed hug and smile at Cricket. "Your mom's right. We'll keep Mrs. Havalin in check. I've dealt with plenty of divas who were a hundred times worse. She won't even know she's being managed."

"That's my girl." Jackie presses a kiss to my forehead, and Cricket giggles. As my aunt releases us, she glances at the shed. "You taking over my she-cave?"

"I should've asked first," I reply with a grimace.

"You're home now. What's ours is yours. Besides, you'll probably get more sleep out here than if you were in the house. Karma's girls are . . . wild. Not that I can say anything." She shakes her head. "I swear, some days it's everything I can do not to toss her out on her ass, but I'd probably never see my grandbabies again, so I don't."

The lines of strain that bracket Jackie's mouth tell me that Karma has put her mom in a difficult position. It's probably too much to think that I can help make that situation better, but I resolve to at least try to talk to my cousin about it if I get the opportunity. *And hope to escape without her biting my head off.*

"She wasn't exactly thrilled to see me either."

Aunt Jackie's crow's-feet deepen, and I hate the defeated expression on her face. "She thinks the world owes her something. I don't know where she got that from, because we all know you don't wish for it—you work for it."

"That doesn't give her an excuse to just up and disappear

on a moment's notice, leaving us scrambling to figure out how to take care of the kids and still make it to our own jobs," Cricket says, her tone bitter.

"Where does she go?"

My aunt shrugs. "No idea. She's about as good at keeping secrets as your mama was." As soon as Jackie says it, her face pales. "I shouldn't have said that. I'm sorry, Whit. You know I didn't mean—"

My stomach twists into a knot because we all know how that ended. "It's okay. Let's just hope Karma's story has a happier ending."

Cricket looks at the ground, and Jackie's gaze darts away from mine.

Awkward silence hangs between us until I clear my throat. "So . . . anyone hiring around here? I could definitely use a job. I'm even willing to wash windows, if that's what's available."

Jackie reaches out to grab my hand and holds it between us. "You haven't scrubbed anything since you left town. Did you really think you would come back home and start cleaning toilets?"

I tug my hand out of her grip. "I just want something normal. Where I can stay out of the way and not be noticed."

She props her hand on a hip. "You mean you want to hide from the world and lick your wounds."

My aunt always knew me better than my own mom, so I may as well confess the truth.

"Exactly."

"That's gonna be tough . . . unless you want to work for the Riscoffs."

The memory of seeing Lincoln earlier today crashes through my system. *Work for them? For* him*?*

"There's got to be another option."

"Not one that pays as well. Think about it. If you want, I'll talk to Ms. Riscoff."

"I'll think about it," I reply, but inside I'm swearing that there's no way in hell I'll ever go down that road.

Before Jackie can push the subject any further, shrieks of "Lala!" come from the back of the house and two little blond girls who look like they could be Cricket and Karma clones come running out.

Jackie turns around to scoop one up in each arm and spins them around. "My babies are home! Tell me all about everything."

Another wave of nostalgia washes over me. She used to say the same thing to Cricket and Karma and me when we'd get home from school.

My own mom had never asked a single question. She was too busy out running around and keeping secrets, just like Jackie said.

But that's all in the past. It's time to move forward.

I swallow the lump in my throat and paste a smile on my face. It's time to meet my little cousins.

LINCOLN

THE UNMISTAKABLE SOUND of someone cocking a shotgun is the last thing I want to hear when I open the door to Commodore's house.

"You piece of shit! That was my trout. I've been waiting to catch him for a goddamned year." Magnus Gable's voice is just as distinctive as the gun.

"Not my fault you're a piss-poor fisherman!"

Another shotgun cocks.

Jesus fucking Christ.

"Hey! Lower the—"

Boom. Boom.

I shove the door open and rush into the house to see Commodore aiming for a second shot from his motorized chair. Blood drips down his face.

"Missed me, you bastard!"

"Sir, you're bleeding!"

Goose hops up off the boards of the deck and trots toward me. The damn dog is a hell of a lot less concerned by the guns being fired than I am.

Commodore shakes his head, splattering blood on the

leather armrest. "Shrapnel. Just a scratch. Gable's buckshot took a chunk out of the goddamn house. Now I'm gonna break his windows."

"Cease fire or I'm calling the cops on both of you!" I yell loud enough so there's no way Magnus can't hear me, even being partially deaf.

"You raised a pussy, Riscoff!" Magnus yells. "My kin would grab a gun and join in!"

I pull out my cell phone, not in the mood to get shot this morning. "Last chance before I dial the sheriff."

Commodore shoots me a cutting look. "Put the damn phone away. You're making me look bad." Blood streams down the side of his face, turning his white beard red.

"Here's the deal—you put the feud on hold for first aid and business, and then you two can go back to shooting each other all you want after I'm gone."

Commodore's glare would frighten the piss out of a lesser man, but I've had enough of this bullshit. I'm not about to let Magnus Gable put a bullet in him today, not when I'm still working out my strategy for going after his grand-niece.

Commodore wipes the blood away from his face and looks down at his hand. "Superglue and duct tape are in the kitchen drawer. I don't need no damn first-aid kit. And mind yourself when you're talking to me. You don't run me, son. I run you. Don't forget it."

My jaw clenches at the reminder. "Maybe I should just let the two of you kill each other, and then I'd have a hell of a lot less problems to deal with."

Commodore sputters as I head for the kitchen.

I respect the man and the sacrifices he made to get Riscoff Holdings to where it is today, but he's living in the past, and by staying there, we're not going to thrive. I spent last night reviewing information on the acquisition I want to make, not only because I was trying to keep my mind off Whitney, but also because we have to diversify again. Otherwise, we're going to wither instead of flourish.

Commodore isn't going to like it. I already know it, but I need his sign-off to enter the auction process to get our hands on one of the most lucrative new tech companies that has the intellectual property we need to revolutionize the next generation of transportation.

I grab a handful of paper towels and yank open drawers in the kitchen to find the old man's supplies. What he needs is a keeper. The last drawer holds a bunch of papers and odds and ends. Superglue is at the front, and I grab and pull out the documents to dig for the duct tape.

I still when my gaze catches on a letter falling out of a manila envelope—with my father's name at the top.

What the hell?

I forget all about the two old men with shotguns pointed at each other and pull it out. Five words stand out in stark relief.

REQUEST FOR A PATERNITY TEST

WHAT THE FUCK?

I scan the rest of the document. It's dated three months ago. The letterhead says it's from a lawyer's office in New York. They want a DNA sample . . . from my deceased father.

Fuck the superglue and the duct tape. Commodore can bleed until he tells me what the hell this is about and why he hasn't mentioned it. I grip the letter and stalk out to the deck, my back to Magnus Gable's house.

"What the fuck is this?" I hold up the paper. "Who wants a paternity test?"

Commodore lowers his shotgun to rest on his lap and turns the chair to face me. "Put that back."

"Not a chance. You need to tell me what the hell is going on. If there's someone who's trying to take a piece of the family holdings because they think it's a get-rich-quick scheme, our lawyers need to shut it down as quick as possible."

Commodore's expression tightens. "It's nobody's damn business but mine."

I study the old man who I've always known to be absolutely ruthless when it comes to his business adversaries, not to mention this stupid feud with the Gables, and something isn't right.

"You should be crushing this person. Why are you hiding it? Do you think there's a chance this is legit?"

His gaze flicks down to the deck. He stows the shotgun more securely and his chair buzzes as it rolls toward me. "We can talk about this inside. Don't need to chance Gable overhearing about our dirty laundry."

I step out of the way as Commodore disappears into the living room. Once we're both inside, I shut the door.

"You do think it's legit then."

He turns around to face me, but his expression is unreadable. He inhales and releases a long breath as one thumb taps on the wooden stock of the shotgun. My brain races faster with every passing moment that he doesn't answer.

"It wasn't like Roosevelt was a saint. Wouldn't be all that surprising if he spread a few bastards around."

Commodore might as well have shot me in the gut. Roosevelt is my father. Or rather, *was*.

"Are you serious?" I've never thought of my father as a

saint. Far from it, but the idea of him having other children isn't something I ever thought I'd have to consider.

What. The. Fuck?

"It's possible," Commodore says simply.

"And what are you doing about it? We need to know. We need to make decisions. Act. Have a strategy."

My mind flies along at a million miles an hour. The Riscoff family succession has never been questioned. From the day I was born, I've been the Riscoff heir. For over 170 years, the company and estate have been handed down to the oldest male descendant, and every other descendant is legally entitled to nothing.

"I've been handling it. Quietly, because I don't want the family name dragged through the dirt again." His gaze narrows on me. "We don't need that."

"You told them they can't get a DNA sample, right?"

Commodore nods slowly, suddenly looking like he's aged twenty years. "They want to exhume the body. Latest letter gave me thirty days to agree before they file a petition with the court."

My head fills with static.

They want to crack open my father's casket. Remove his body. All to see if there's another potential Riscoff heir who could claim the family's assets.

This is not happening.

"Jesus fucking Christ." My voice comes out rough as I shake my head. I meet the old man's gaze. "What did they say when you told them no way in hell?"

He lifts his chin. "I haven't replied. I'm still thinking on it."

I blink twice, staring at him like I don't understand the language he's speaking. "You've got to be fucking kidding me."

"Don't you take that tone with me, boy. I make the decisions." He grips both arms of his chair. "We don't need this in court. How do you think that would make us look? And your mother? She'd lose her goddamn mind."

The reality of the situation hits me. If they dig up my father, my mother is going to have a heart attack. Maybe not literally, but close enough. She could never handle this. But why would Commodore Riscoff, the man who refuses to be forced into anything, allow this?

"They wanted a settlement and you said no, didn't you?"

He nods sharply. "That's when they came back with the exhumation request."

"Fuck. They must think this person is truly my father's son, and older than me. That's the only way it makes financial sense to pursue it." I meet the old man's gaze. "You want to hand everything over to a complete stranger? Someone who hasn't worked himself to the bone for the last decade to *protect and preserve your legacy*?"

Commodore's gaze turns flinty. "I don't like any of it. And I haven't kicked the bucket yet. I can change my will anytime I want. You'd do well to remember that, boy. I still get to decide who gets what. No family tradition binds me if I change my mind."

My head drops back and I stare up at the wood-plank ceiling, desperately trying to find control amidst the chaos that has just been unleashed on my life. When I've gathered myself, I meet the old man's dark brown eyes.

"What do you want me to do? Because we can make this go away. They need a court order for the exhumation."

His jaw clenches. "I haven't decided what I want to do yet. But it'd make me feel a hell of a lot better if I knew the family line was going to continue."

I stare at him, unsure why I'm shocked, but I am. "That's

how you're going to play this? You want me to knock up some woman and hope it's a boy so you can feel good about the family line continuing?"

His lips flatten and his stare turns hard. "Marry whoever that woman is before you knock her up."

"I've played your games for years." I take a step toward him, my hands balled into fists. "I've done everything you've ever asked of me, but I draw the line here."

Heavy silence hangs between us before Commodore leans back in his chair.

"You don't want to see to making sure we have a new generation of Riscoffs? Then there's no reason for me not to find out who this other heir might be."

My teeth threaten to shatter from the intensity of my jaw clenching. When I've got a grip on the rage coursing through my veins, I finally speak. "That's how you're going to play it?"

Commodore smiles like he's Niccolò Machiavelli himself. "You'll fall in line. You always do. Just make sure it's not that Gable girl."

LINCOLN

The past

"When can I see you again?" I asked.

Whitney Gable lay wrapped in my arms in the bedroom of the cabin, and I didn't want to let her go. Her body stiffened. She was already drawing back, and I didn't like it.

"We can't keep doing this. If someone finds out—"

"No one is going to find out."

Her blue eyes narrowed as her expression turned mulish. She was way too fucking cute for her own good. My dick, which should have been permanently out of commission after how many rounds we'd already gone, came back to life.

"Looking at me like that doesn't make me want to see you any less."

"You can't say that no one will find out. My aunt already saw you. She knows something's up."

"And is she going to tell anyone?"

Whitney shook her head. "Aunt Jackie wouldn't do that, but that's not my point. My point is that we *already got caught*. It's bound to happen again. This town is too small."

I rolled her onto her back and settled between her legs.

"So you're saying you don't want any more of this?" I nudged my cock against her opening, and she was already wet for me.

Whitney arched in the bed, teasing me until I pushed inside. Immediately, she shoved at my shoulders.

"Condom. We need a condom."

I groaned because she felt so fucking good without one. But she was right. We did need one. All it would take was once . . . and that would be something we couldn't hide. Which would almost be a relief.

I rolled off her and reached for the last one on the nightstand. I had never gone through this many rubbers in a night, but with Whitney, I couldn't get enough. She was the most addictive drug ever to hit my system. When I thought about her, it was a constant push for *more, more, more.*

After sliding on the condom, I settled back between her legs and pushed inside. It was still fucking amazing, but I knew damn well nothing could compare to going bare with her.

Something I'd never done before.

Commodore and my dad had drilled it into my head—women will try anything to get knocked up with a potential Riscoff heir, and I'd seen enough evidence to believe it. Whitney making me use a condom once again told me she was different.

She wanted nothing from me except maybe my dick and the orgasms I gave her, and even those might be in jeopardy.

"You know we'd figure it out if something happened. I'd take care of you."

Whitney's blue eyes widened. "Don't say that. Do you know what would happen if something . . . happened? My family would disown me. And then your family? I don't even want to think about it. They'd run me out of town on a rail. Probably take out a hit. Taint the Riscoff line with Gable blood? Your mother would hack me into pieces, after she ran me over with a car and shot me a dozen times."

Whitney was right. My mother would go ballistic if she knew about this. She would lose her goddamned mind. I would never hear the end of it. Ever.

A smile curled my lips.

It wouldn't be the end of the world, though.

"I'd protect you from her. I wouldn't let any of them touch you."

Whitney placed a finger over my lips to stop me from saying anything else. "We're not talking about this. Stop putting shit like that out into the universe. If you mention it again, I *will* refuse to see you again."

"Fine." I kissed her finger before I thrust inside her. We both let out harsh groans.

"How is it always so good?" she said, moaning and arching her back.

I shifted so I was on my knees, never losing contact. "Because we're fucking perfect together."

Her blue gaze collided with mine before she rolled her eyes. "You say that to all the girls."

"It's never been like this before. *Never*," I told her with a shake of my head. "I'm not lying. No bullshit."

Her skeptical look faded when I started to move, and I could already feel her muscles fluttering around me. I'd only had two nights with her, but I'd made a study of her body like I was going to be tested on it. Learning what she liked. What made her go off like the Fourth of July. It was my most favorite subject of all time.

By the time she'd come twice, I unloaded into the condom, and Whitney dozed off for a few minutes after we cleaned up. I wrapped myself around her naked body again, and I couldn't help but think about keeping her. Making her mine. Saying *fuck the feud*. My family. Her family.

She's different.

She wanted me despite who I was. That meant something to me, and I didn't want to lose it.

That was when I decided exactly how I'd prevent it from happening.

I'm going to make her fall in love with me.

WHITNEY

Present day

MY FIRST NIGHT in the she-shed turned into a sleepover with Cricket, and that was totally fine by me. At least, until she had to leave at the ass crack of dawn to lead a hike up into the mountains, and I couldn't fall back to sleep.

Being home unsettles me.

With Cricket's bright chatter around, it's easy to block out thoughts of Lincoln, but as soon as I'm left with silence, everything about him and our history comes rushing back.

For ten years, I've been telling myself my memory made too much of it. That it wasn't as good as I remember. That's what I needed to tell myself to get through the days of being Ricky Rango's wife.

I never should have married him.

But at the time, there was no other choice. I'd only agreed to marry him if he stayed true to his promise to be faithful. And shockingly, he did.

At least until I went in for my annual physical earlier this year, and my doctor delivered the bad news that I had an

STD. Antibiotics might have fixed the medical part of it . . . but absolutely nothing could change the fact that my marriage was over.

When I confronted Ricky, he blamed me. Said I must have gotten it from cheating on *him*. That accusation caught me completely off guard, and I knew it had to be coming from the guilt. Monogamy was the one thing he promised me in return for everything I did for him. *The only thing.*

I should have known he couldn't keep that promise.

My world revolved around his career. Going wherever his tour took us. Making sure he never disappointed his fans. Keeping him off drugs and away from damaging publicity.

He'd been careful; I'd give him that. He hadn't gotten caught by the paparazzi. But that didn't change a thing.

I refused to be *that* woman. I wasn't going to give him another day of my life when he refused to treat me with the most basic level of respect, and had been lying to me for who knows how long.

I'll still never forget his face when I told him it was over and I was filing for divorce.

Absolutely stunned shock.

Then came the rage. His screams that I would never humiliate him like that.

I stayed stoic. Refused to back down.

That's when he turned cruel.

I can still hear his words ringing in my head. *"I don't know why you care now. I've been fucking around for ten years. I never loved you. I needed you. There's a difference."*

Then I played my trump card. I told him he'd give me a quick and quiet divorce, or I'd tell the truth and everyone would know what a fraud he'd always been.

His temper detonated and he charged me. I ran for the

safe room and locked him out. He pounded on it for an hour, threatening to kill me if I ever told.

When he gave up, he destroyed everything in his path on the way out—furniture, mirrors, art, walls, doors.

Crying, I called Cricket. She wanted to call the police, but I refused. Instead, I waited hours before coming out—until I saw pictures people posted, tagging him at a hotel and saying he was throwing a massive party.

I packed as fast as I could and got the hell out of the house before he could come back. I was holed up in a hotel in San Diego the next day when I got the call from the police. They needed me to identify his body.

I roll over on the futon and close my eyes, picturing the videos of hordes of angry fans screaming outside our front gate as soon as the news broke. Their signs. Their messages. The death threats.

All because they said I'd killed a legend in the making.

No one cared that Ricky's own hand held the needle that carried the fatal dose of heroin and fentanyl.

No one cared that I wasn't there when it happened.

No one cared about anything but Ricky Rango and the story he spun for them before he died. The story where I was the evil cheating whore of a wife who was out to destroy him and his music.

My shoulders begin to shake as the memories threaten to break me.

No. Not today. Not ever again.

I throw off the quilt and bolt out of bed. *I gave him everything for ten years of my life, and I will not give him a single second more.*

I have a new life to get in order, and not one single part of it will have anything to do with Ricky Rango beyond the stack of cash shoved in my purse. That was all I took when I left, besides my clothes, and I was lucky that I had squirreled away some household petty cash in the event of a rainy day. Ricky's financial manager met with me before the funeral to inform me that there was no money left due to Ricky's outrageous spending habits.

I reach for my purse and count out the bills.

Four thousand six hundred and nineteen dollars. It's not going to last me long, even though Gable is cheaper than LA.

I need to find a way to pay my own way. I'm thirty-one, infamously widowed, and have no marketable job skills for a town like Gable besides being a half-decent cleaning lady a decade ago.

Flopping back on the bed, I squeeze my eyes shut and think about what the hell someone here might pay me to do.

Working for the Riscoffs is out of the question. My pride won't let me . . . at least, not unless I'm starving.

Lead wilderness hikes with Cricket? I'd get lost five minutes into the woods.

I have no idea what Karma does, but there's no way I can work with her.

Which leaves coffee shops, bars, and other places Ricky's fans could easily get to me. I touch my cheek where my black eye is probably fading into an awesome purplish green.

No. I can't make myself an easy target.

While I'm contemplating what the hell I'm going to do with my life, someone bangs on the door. I jump, grabbing the stack of money and shoving it under a pillow, just in case it's Karma.

"You up, Whit?" It's Aunt Jackie.

"Yeah, one sec." I hurry to the door and pull it open. "Sorry, getting a bit of a late start this morning. Cricket and I talked half the night."

Jackie's answering smile shines brilliantly enough to light

up the dreary morning. "She left a note on the counter telling me that having you home was the best wedding present she could ask for."

I wrap my arms around my middle and smile. "I'm glad me coming home makes at least a couple people happy."

"You've got two people firmly in that camp, and I'm sure a whole lot more." She narrows her gaze on me, and I flinch as she reaches a hand toward my face. "Hey, calm down. Just want to see that eye of yours. I thought you did a half-assed job covering it, but you've got a doozy of a bruise. Who do I need to kill?"

"He got arrested, and I pressed charges. If they want me to come back to LA to testify, I might have to drop the case."

Aunt Jackie's mouth screws tight. "Oh, hell no. We'll go back together and teach that bastard a lesson."

"Hopefully it won't come to that, but I appreciate it." Her ferocity in my defense makes my eye hurt a little less.

"That's family. It's what we do. Speaking of family . . . are you going to your parents'—"

I shake my head. "No. I can't. Not yet."

Jackie sighs but there's not much she can say. She can't make me deal with things I refuse to deal with.

"Okay. Well, I was coming out here to see if you wanted to sneak into the resort with me today and use up some of my spa credits I get for bonuses. You look like you could use a day of pampering. Maybe they can cover up that bruise a little better for you too. Or even put some fancy stuff on your face to heal it faster. I don't do facials, but everyone raves about the girls there."

In my former life, facials were a regular thing, but I don't expect to continue partaking in them now.

"I don't need all that. I'm fine. You should use them on yourself. Or save them for Cricket for the wedding."

"I've got tons of credits. If I was gonna use them myself, I would've. I already blocked off a chunk for you girls for the wedding too." She eyes me skeptically. "Don't tell me you couldn't use a few hours of relaxation. Maybe a massage to help work out some of that tension you're holding on to so tightly."

She's not wrong, but . . .

"It's a Riscoff resort."

Jackie tilts her head to the right. "Put that out of your mind and get dressed. I'm not taking no for an answer. Anyway, I'm guessing you'd rather spend the day on Riscoff property rather than listening to Karma slam doors and blare music while the girls are gone. According to the neighbors, that might as well be her job instead of that online stuff she does."

Well, that answers one question about what Karma does for work. And no, I don't want to be around her any more than I have to be, at least until her attitude calms down.

"Fine. You win. I'll be ready in ten."

WHITNEY

THE DRIVE UP to The Gables takes twenty minutes. It's perched on the side of a mountain overlooking the river that cuts through the gorge. Ricky once played at the Biltmore Estate in North Carolina, and I wondered if the Riscoffs felt inadequate, so they had to try to build something even more grand. It's over two hundred thousand square feet, and I don't even want to think about how much it cost to build.

It's also only a few miles down the road from the Riscoff estate. *But I won't be going anywhere near that place.*

Actually, I can't believe I'm even daring to go to The Gables.

Aunt Jackie guides the car past the front gate and turns down a road that leads around the side. I stare at the structure silently as we pass by it. I would love to call it a monstrosity, but instead it's like something out of a fairy tale. It looks like a French chateau on crack that should have a prince and princess presiding over it. But the Riscoffs rule here.

I attempt to put that fact out of my brain, but it's pointless. I'll never forget that.

Aunt Jackie slows before a black gate around the rear and

waves her security badge at a card reader before it slides open.

"I'll show you to the spa, and then get to work. They always keep a few appointment slots open at all times for VIPs. If you finish before me, you can take the car home and come back to get me at six."

VIPs? That's what I used to be, but I'm definitely not anymore.

"Are you sure this is a good idea? I don't want you to get in trouble."

"Shush. Ms. Riscoff wants her employees to be happy, and this makes me happy. I'm not getting in trouble for anything unless I don't get inside and get to my desk in the next sixteen minutes."

As Jackie parks the car, I get a view of the back of the resort and the towering shrubs that surround the garden maze.

The garden maze I'll never forget because of Lincoln.

WHITNEY

The past

"Where are we going?"

"Keep your eyes closed."

It was a miracle that I'd agreed to the blindfold, and probably a sign I should have been questioning my sanity. But Lincoln had a surprise, and he talked me into going along with it while holding out on letting me come. *He plays dirty in bed.*

From beneath the cloth over my eyes, everything was dark, and I was terrified someone was going to see us together, even though he promised he wouldn't let that happen. He didn't seem to understand how big of a disaster it would be if we got caught. I couldn't imagine dealing with the fallout. Maybe his attitude was different because he was used to having power, and I was used to having none. Either way, I couldn't risk it.

"Okay. You can look now."

I pulled the blindfold off and found we were surrounded by walls of green. "Where are we?"

"The maze."

I looked at him like he was crazy. "What maze? Where?"

"The Gables. I used to play here as a kid. It was—"

"You brought me to The Gables?" I covered my mouth to cut off my screech. In a much quieter tone, I asked, "Why would you do that?"

The excitement faded from his features. "Because you won't let me take you on a damned date, and as much as I would love to stay in bed and do nothing but fuck you, you deserve better."

The simple words of his statement hit me hard in a place I'd been keeping armored against him.

"You can't say things like that to me," I whispered, looking away.

Lincoln's fingers lifted my chin. "I can and I will. We're both better than that."

"I can't—"

"I know. And that's why we're here. Unless it's a garden party night, the maze is usually empty. It's fine. We're safe."

I wanted to believe him, but my apprehension wouldn't completely fade. Still, when he looked at me like that, like he thought I was worth so much more than I could ever conceive, it made me feel things I shouldn't. It also made me let him have his way.

"Fine." I conceded and leaned forward to press a kiss to his lips. "You win."

Lincoln's smile seemed to brighten the entire world. "If all it takes is a million-dollar garden to make you kiss me outside the walls of the cabin, then I'll bring you here every day."

Instead of focusing on the sweetness he kept dishing out, I latched onto the other part of the statement. "A million dollars? Are you serious?"

He shrugged. "Maybe. My great-grandmother went over the top when she expanded it."

I couldn't even comprehend that much money. Or how easily Lincoln talked about it. That was one thing that would always separate us like an impenetrable wall.

I was broke. He was richer than sin.

"Come on. I didn't just bring you here to stand around. We're going to play a game." His smile morphed into a mischievous grin I knew I wouldn't be able to resist.

Why am I so weak when it comes to him? I decided I didn't care right now. I just wanted to keep that look on his face.

"What kind of game?"

"I'm going to give you a head start to find the center, and you're going to leave me clues about which direction you take."

"Clues?"

"In the form of clothes."

I jerked back. "Oh, hell no. Not happening."

"You always say that . . . but eventually you change your mind."

He took my hand, but I pulled it free and poked him in the chest with my index finger. "Not this time, rich boy. You wanna play that game, you're stripping."

Lincoln's smile widened. "Fine. But when you find me naked, I'm not going to be responsible for what happens."

Somehow, against all odds, a flutter of excitement built inside me, even though objectively I knew this was a terrible idea.

Indecision warred in my brain, and Lincoln, who read me way too accurately, must have seen it.

"Give me a two-minute head start, and don't you dare

leave me here alone, Blue." He pulled me against him and took my lips in a hard kiss.

I swallowed, still second-guessing this, but I repeated his words. "Two-minute head start."

His grin widened. "Just so you know, you're the most fun I've ever had."

Before I could reply, or even absorb the words fully, he disappeared into the maze.

As soon as he was out of sight, my reservations came flooding back.

This is the best worst plan ever. We're going to get caught. With Lincoln naked.

And yet, I counted to 120 and darted in the direction he went. Within fifty feet, I hit a fork.

Shit. Which way? I peered down each path and spotted a shoe down one. A smile tugged at my lips as I imagined Lincoln dropping it for me.

Maybe this is kind of fun.

I ran to the shoe and grabbed it, heading down the corridor of hedges, excited to hit another choice. When I did, I found another shoe. And then a sock. Another sock.

Then his shirt.

Now we're talking.

My man liked to go commando, so there might not be much left now.

I froze where I stood.

My man?

What the hell?

Uh. No. He's not my man. He's a fling. That's it. That's all. It's just a rebound. A forbidden rebound.

Even as I told myself this, I knew I was lying.

Lincoln Riscoff had already turned me into an addict, and I was dangerously close to feeling things about him that I shouldn't be feeling. He'd cast a spell on me . . . otherwise, there was no way I'd be standing in the maze at The Gables right now. Before I could think more on it, I heard a whisper.

"Blue, I'm starting to get cold over here."

My head jerked to the right and everything faded away except for the knowledge that Lincoln was naked and not far away.

I wasted no time heading for the shorts I saw on the ground, but before I could reach them, Lincoln's arms wrapped around me and he picked me up from behind. A burst of laughter broke free from my lips as the clothes and shoes I'd gathered dropped to the grass.

"A little eager to find me?"

"You're naked, aren't you?"

His breath was hot against my ear. "Is that all you want from me? My body? Shame on you. You know I'm more than that."

I did know, and that was the problem.

I swallowed and turned in his arms. "I sure don't want you for your name or your money."

Once again, I succeeded in sucking the lightheartedness out of the moment. Lincoln's features darkened, but not with anger.

"That's one of my most favorite things about you."

His mouth crushed against mine, and he devoured me. I lost track of how long he kissed me, standing naked there in that maze. My hands were everywhere, skating over his hard muscles as I gripped his shoulders.

"I want you," I whispered.

"Who's there?" a man called out.

We both went silent. I attempted to tug out of Lincoln's arms, but he held me tight.

"Lincoln Riscoff. Who's asking?" There was something

about the confident way he said his name that made it clear he didn't expect to be challenged.

I pulled harder and he finally released me as someone came around the corner of the final hedge that led to the center of the maze, and I ducked behind Lincoln's back.

"Sorry, sir. Didn't expect to see you . . . I'll just be going then."

I recognized the voice. It was a guy my aunt Jackie dated occasionally. He was a groundskeeper here. *Shit.*

"And you won't be mentioning this to anyone either, will you?"

"No, sir. Of course not, sir."

I could picture him trying to sneak a glimpse over Lincoln's shoulder to identify who was with him, so I didn't risk a look.

We heard him shuffle away, and I stayed huddled until Lincoln turned around. I immediately stepped back and reached down to grab the pile of clothes and throw them at him.

"We have to go. Now. Right now. We can't—"

Lincoln yanked on his shorts and snagged my wrist to pull me back into his arms. "Stop panicking. It's fine. He's not going to say a word. If he does, he knows he'll lose his job."

"But—"

"Whitney. Stop." Lincoln didn't usually use my name, and it got my attention more effectively than anything else would in that moment. "I'm not going to let anyone find out about us. Nothing bad is going to happen to you because we're together. I promise."

His gaze said he was sincere, but in this, I wasn't ready to trust his confidence.

"You can't promise that. We both know this isn't going to end well. It can't."

His expression darkened. "We decide how this ends. Only us. And unless you tell me right now that I mean nothing to you, I'm not letting you go."

I opened my mouth to say the words that would set me free from this craziness and save me from self-destruction, but nothing came out. The thought of never seeing him again made me sick to my stomach.

"You can't say it. I know you can't, even if you want to be able to. I see you, Whitney. I see you so fucking clearly that I never want to look at anyone else ever again. Do you get what I'm saying?"

I dropped my forehead to press against his bare chest and breathed in the pine-and-citrus scent of his skin. "I'm scared."

His arms wrapped around me, and he pressed me tightly enough against his strong body that I actually thought he could protect me from the world.

"You don't need to be scared, Blue. You have me."

WHITNEY

Present day

I HAVEN'T FELT this relaxed in months. After a massage and a facial that made me feel like a new woman, I'm led to the makeup station to cover this awesome bruise on my face.

When I walk inside, I'm shocked to see someone I recognize. "Gabi?"

"Whitney? Jesus, it's been like a million years." She rushes forward to give me a hug.

I've gotten more hugs in the last couple of days than I have in the past decade, and something about it makes me feel really, really good. I didn't know how much I missed being around people who knew me as someone other than *Ricky Rango's wife*.

"More like a million and one. I didn't know you moved back."

Gabi was one of my closest friends in high school, but we lost touch when she went away to college and I stayed in Gable, waiting for Ricky to hit it big in LA.

"About two years ago. I got divorced and didn't want to

raise my kids anywhere near that asshole, so here I am. Thirty-two and living with mom and dad. Winning at life, you know?"

I smile. "I'm moving back in with my aunt. I think we're both killing it."

Her smile fades when she flips on the bright light of the makeup station and sees the bruise on my face. "Speaking of killing, who needs to die for doing that?"

Warmth bursts inside me. It's also been a long time since I've had people in my life who would help me bury a body without question.

"It's a long, boring story that I'm working hard to move on from. Right now, I'd rather cover it up and pretend it never happened."

"I feel you, girl. My ex hit me once. That was the last straw. I got full custody because of all those pictures I took. It was worth it to never let him see my babies again without supervision."

I reach out and squeeze her hand. "I'm so sorry you had to go through that."

"That's life. We get the shit and the good. It's up to us how long we take the shit. I thought I heard you were going to get divorced before . . . before your husband died." Her statement carries the hint of a question, and I nod.

I know the story will follow me everywhere I go for the rest of my life, so I may as well get used to hearing it. "You probably heard that I killed him too."

Gabi's gaze dips before meeting mine again. "I did, but I didn't believe it."

"That makes you one of very few. I wasn't even there when it happened. But his fans will never believe it. They want me to be the villain in this story."

"I'm sorry you had to deal with that. You'd think being

married to a rock star would be great . . ." She glances at my eye again. "But obviously everything has its drawbacks."

I nod. "The press and the fans are still crazy, but I'm hoping they won't track me back here. At least, for a little while."

"No one will hear you're home from me. Cross my heart." She draws an *X* over her heart like we used to do when we were younger.

"I appreciate that."

"Enough of that and on to business." Gabi lifts my chin with two fingers and surveys my face. "Let's get this covered up and make you so damn hot that Lincoln Riscoff won't know what the hell happened to him when he sees you."

I freeze at the mention of his name. "You know about . . . that?"

"I don't think there's a single person in this town who doesn't know about him objecting at your wedding. It's the stuff of legend." She pauses to take a breath. "I'm sure everyone would *love* to see you snake him away from that bitch who thinks she's got her claws into him now. We can tell she's nothing but a gold digger, but for some reason, Mrs. Riscoff seems to approve. I was definitely betting on her keeling over if Lincoln thought about getting engaged to another woman who didn't meet her standards."

Another woman?

"He was engaged before?" I have no idea why my brain latches onto that piece of information, but clearly, it's demented.

Also, *how did I not know Lincoln was engaged?* Oh, wait, because I've been pretending Lincoln Riscoff and the entire town of Gable didn't exist for ten years while being wrapped up trying to make sure Ricky's career continued to skyrocket.

"Almost, but then she got caught in bed with his brother, so she didn't get a ring."

"What?" My exclamation bounces around the room.

"It was scandalous. Mrs. Riscoff ended up in the hospital from chest pains, but that old bat is never gonna die, if you ask me. She's determined to see the next Riscoff heir being born before she leaves this earth."

I have nothing I can say to that statement, because *holy shit*, I did miss a hell of a lot. I swallow my shock.

"Here, scoot forward on the chair. I'll tell you the story while I work."

Part of me wants to say I don't care, but who am I kidding? Of course I want to hear this. It's pretty much impossible not to want to know everything that happened in my absence involving Lincoln.

As Gabi smooths primer onto my face, I ask, "And the gold digger this time is Maren something?" I ask like I didn't commit the name of the woman Cricket almost ran off the road to memory.

"Maren Higgins. She's a piece of work too. Already thinks she's lady of the manor, although she's not, because Lincoln doesn't live at the Riscoff estate and hasn't in ages. Thankfully, Ms. Riscoff told her she can't come in here and order us around unless she pays full price, so she's not around too often. She's from the city. Her family sounds fancy, but the kind of fancy that needs a cash infusion. Lord knows when she lost her chance at Hunter Havalin, she moved right up the food chain because the Riscoffs have plenty of cash. I'm not sure why she didn't go after him first, but craftier women than her have set their sights on Lincoln Riscoff and failed. Although, I still have no idea why he wanted to marry Monica. I don't think anyone understands that."

Gabi is laying out so much information right now that I'm

struggling to absorb it all . . . while stomping out tiny flames of jealousy I'm pretending don't exist.

He's not mine. He never will be. I don't care. This is just entertaining gossip. That's all.

I'm full of shit.

"So Monica is the ex who slept with Harrison. How long ago was that?" I ask like I'm making idle conversation, but I'm wildly curious.

"I missed out on the Monica era, but from what I've been told, it was only a few years after you left town. By the way . . . she had black hair, blue eyes, and a body straight out of Victoria's Secret."

I freeze as Gabi goes to work on my brows.

Black hair and blue eyes? No coincidence there at all . . .

"And Maren?" I try to change the subject immediately. "What does she look like?"

"The kind of woman you love to hate. Blond. Tiny waist. Great boobs. Legs that go on for days. Perma-tan. Gorgeous and she knows it."

"Sounds . . . lovely." I place sarcastic emphasis on *lovely*.

"Oh, Whit. God, you should see her. It's like she's Regina George out of *Mean Girls*. She has this attitude that only comes out when she's nowhere near Lincoln. The one time I did her makeup, I thought about dumping something in the foundation to give her an allergic reaction, because she was so awful. If I wouldn't have gotten fired, I would have done it in a heartbeat."

"Yikes."

"Yeah, he sure can pick some winners. At least he's kept it from getting too serious. It's more off-again these days than anything. If you ask me, he's just using her as a booty call. Poor woman thinks that's how to nab the Riscoff heir. She's crazy, if you ask me. He won't buy what he can get for free, and that man can get *everything* for free."

Her words stab into me.

He got it for free from me too . . . and he still wanted more.

"Do you want me to go natural on your eyes or sultry?" Gabi asks, holding an eyeshadow palette aloft as another spa employee comes in with a woman wrapped in a robe and sandals on her feet. They set up at the station on the opposite side of the room.

"Natural is fine. I don't need glam treatment. It's not like I'm getting fixed up to go anywhere."

"No, but you never know who you're gonna see . . ."

We both know exactly who she's talking about, and I don't even want to contemplate what's going to happen the next time I see Lincoln. Even having glass between us and me pretending he wasn't there was more than I could handle.

I wish seeing him once had proven that I don't care anymore, but all it proved was that I've been lying to myself for years. My body roared to life like I've been sleepwalking for the last ten years.

I shove all that aside and focus on the task at hand. "As long as you cover up my fabulous black eye, I'll be fine."

Gabi's bubbly attitude fades in the face of the harsh reality of why I'm here. "You going to tell me where you buried him? The guy who hit you?"

"I pressed charges. I'm hoping I never have to see him again."

"Good girl. Someday, you and I are going to go out, have some drinks, and catch up. Sounds like we both need it." She pauses for a moment. "And just so you know, no one in this town had any great love for Ricky. I guarantee they aren't blaming you for what happened."

It takes everything I have to keep my smile pasted on my face and not let the tears gathering spill.

"Thank you. That means a lot to me."

"Of course, Whit. You're among friends now."

She hands me a tissue, and I carefully dab at my eyes.

"It's been a while since I could talk to anyone who didn't have an ulterior motive. I thought I'd made some good friends in LA, but then I was shocked to find the things I'd told them show up in gossip magazines."

Gabi's brush hand stills. "Those whores. I hope they get crotch rot."

My lips quirk into a rueful smile. "Right? Up until then, no one knew he'd ever been to rehab . . . but they sure spilled that fast."

"You stuck by him through rehab too? God, I didn't know that."

"We managed to keep it out of the press because I covered for him. As far as they know, it was our second honeymoon retreat in Fiji."

"I read about that! So you didn't even go to Fiji?"

"No. I stayed in the house for six weeks without leaving because I couldn't be spotted without screwing up our story."

"It sounds like you made some serious sacrifices for that man."

I shrugged. "Isn't that what marriage is about? Sacrifices?"

"I'm done with all that shit," Gabi says. "Now, it's all about me and my babies."

"Amen."

"You know, except for the necessary bump and grind here and there, I try to keep it real quiet." She pauses. "You know any Hollywood types who need a fling on the side? I'm all about the long-distance relationships." When I laugh, she smiles. "Never mind. I couldn't handle their drama."

"Trust me, you don't want a damn thing to do with that. They're all fake as hell."

She holds the palette up. "Speaking of fake as hell, let's make you so naturally beautiful that Lincoln will forget all about Maren the second he sees your gorgeous face."

"What is she doing here?"

A voice I wish I could forget cuts through the room, and I look up to see Mrs. Riscoff standing in the doorway.

LINCOLN

The past

"Who was she?" My mother slammed the door behind her as she stormed into my father's office in the middle of our meeting.

"Excuse me?" my father said.

"That whore he saw you with!"

I go still. *That piece-of-shit groundskeeper* . . .

"Who the hell are you talking about?" my father asked.

Instead of my mother telling my father what I'd done, she walked by me on the way to slap her hands on his desk.

"My brother said he saw you with a woman last night. Leaving the resort out the back way."

A rush of relief hit me when I realized it wasn't me she was accusing. Even though I'd told Whitney I would handle everything and nothing would touch her, the idea of my mother finding out wasn't something that brought out any warm, fuzzy feelings.

"Then your brother should've realized I was taking an employee home. She had a sick kid and needed a ride."

"At ten o'clock at night? Like I believe that! I checked already, and you had a room blocked off last night."

"I always have a room blocked off. It's so I can work all the damn time and make the company more money. You like money, don't you, Sylvia? That's why you married me, after all."

"You hardly ever come home at night anymore!"

"Why would I when all you do is accuse me of cheating on you all the time?"

I stood and backed up toward the door. The last thing I wanted to do was stand around and listen to my parents argue. They didn't love each other. Never had. I still found it shocking they managed to have three children, because they'd lived in separate wings of the house for as long as I could remember.

I slipped out the door and shut it behind me, muffling their voices a little.

Commodore stepped out of his office, no doubt drawn by the shouting. He glanced at the door and then back at me. "Running away?"

I met his gaze. "Do you want to go in there?"

"Your father is a grown man. He shouldn't have to explain himself to her. But you should learn something from this, boy. Never marry a woman you don't trust or who doesn't trust you. Everything will go to shit faster than you can say *I do*."

The first woman who popped into my head was Whitney. She didn't trust me.

No, that wasn't true. She didn't *want* to trust me, but I was wearing her down. I could trust her . . . at least, I thought I could. I needed to get her to the point where her family loyalty paled in comparison to what she felt for me. That was the only way it would ever work between us.

Which meant I had a long way to go.

Commodore, the canny old man, noticed my silence and narrowed his gaze on me. "You have someone in mind already?"

I shook my head. "Not yet, sir."

I hated the lie, but it wasn't time to tell him yet. Although, if it were up to Whitney, it never would be.

One step at a time. That was how I had to work this.

My mother slammed my father's office door and stopped in front of Commodore. "If your son doesn't learn how to keep his hands to himself, your family is going to have its first ever divorce."

Commodore stood even taller as his gaze hardened. "You'll never walk away from a penny of this voluntarily. But I would write you a check if you do. For a dollar."

My mother inhaled sharply at Commodore's insult. It was harsh enough that it even shocked me.

"Sir—"

He held up a hand to silence me. "You have anything else to add to the conversation, Sylvia?"

My mother glared and stalked away.

Commodore turned back to me when she disappeared into the elevator. "Sometimes you have to take a hard line with the ones who would walk all over you. I know she's your mother, but I don't like that woman."

My father's office door opened and he stepped out. With his hands shoved in his pockets, he asked, "Anyone else need a drink?"

WHITNEY

Present day

"WHAT ARE YOU DOING HERE?" Sylvia Riscoff's question rings with disbelief and disgust.

"Mrs. Riscoff—" Gabi says, but Lincoln's mother whips out her hand to silence her.

"I want an explanation for your presence, and I want it now." Hatred drips from Mrs. Riscoff's every word. It's surprising acid doesn't leak from the corners of her mouth to accompany it.

She despises me. If looks could kill, I'd be dead.

"I'm getting my makeup done." I say it matter-of-factly. "It's an excellent facility."

Her nostrils flare in anger. "A facility you'll never set foot in again. Get out. Your money's no good here."

"Actually, she's here on employee credit, ma'am," Gabi says, not realizing she just threw my aunt into the crosshairs.

"Which employee?"

I swallow. "My aunt."

"I'll have her job for this. You're trash, all of you Gables.

Always have been, always will be. I don't care how much money you have now; it doesn't change who you are."

I blink twice at her. *She thinks I still have money?* I'm not going to correct her, though. It's a mistake that's no doubt in my favor.

"I'm afraid it was approved by me in advance, Mother. We welcome everyone here at The Gables."

A petite brunette wearing a tailored skirt suit steps into the room. She has to be McKinley Riscoff, even though she looks nothing like the shy girl I remember.

"And if you would, please try to keep your voice down in the spa. People are enjoying the tranquility."

"*You* approved this?"

Mrs. Riscoff looks like she's about to have a fit. Her cheeks are turning red, and I'm terrified she's going to drop dead right here in the spa, and then I'll be the Black Widow *and* the Mother Killer.

"I'm almost done, Mrs. Riscoff. I'm sure there will be no reason for me to return after today."

"Oh no, by all means," McKinley says. "You're very welcome here. In fact, I came down to welcome you person-ally. It's not every day we have someone so—"

"Infamous. That's what she is. If nothing else, she'll be terrible for publicity after she drove her husband to kill himself." Mrs. Riscoff spits out the accusations that are no worse than anything I've heard before, but they sting more coming from her. She turns to McKinley. "If that's how you're going to run this resort, I'm sure your grandfather would be happy to take it back and give it to Harrison. He's the one who should've had it to begin with."

McKinley smiles sweetly, but I sense that the girl has her own well-honed suit of armor when it comes to dealing with her mother. "I apologize for my mother's behavior. You're welcome anytime. All you have to do is call, and we'll make sure we can find room for you on the schedule." She turns to Mrs. Riscoff. "Mother, if you'd come with me, there's another matter we need to discuss."

She leads Mrs. Riscoff away, and both Gabi and I breathe a sigh of relief.

"Good Lord. She's a dragon. You dodged a bullet not ending up with her for a mother-in-law. Can you imagine?"

I shiver at the thought. That's something that Mrs. Riscoff *never* would have let happen.

My train of thought is derailed when we hear McKinley scream from the hallway.

"Someone call 911!"

WHITNEY

The past

"Meet me in the hallway on the third floor in twenty minutes."

I knew I shouldn't be in this house. I couldn't stop looking over my shoulder, even though I had a perfectly good reason to be here.

The Riscoffs' housekeeper brought in reinforcements to scrub the entire estate top to bottom before some big party they were hosting tomorrow night, and through some insane turn of events, Aunt Jackie got the offer and snapped up the chance because the pay was so good.

Lincoln had seen me washing floor-to-ceiling windows in the parlor an hour after we got here, and whispered those words in my ear with one of the other household staff only a half a room away working on the chandelier.

Words that I should ignore if I know what's good for me.

It had been two months of clandestine meetings, and every single time, I told myself it was the last time.

I'm a big, fat liar.

I couldn't quit him. I wanted to. I needed to. But I couldn't.

I looked around and saw that the woman in the black-and-white maid's uniform, which thankfully we didn't have to wear, was fixated on cleaning each individual piece of crystal before replacing it.

I could sneak away. I could meet him. But I shouldn't. Every thought I had about Lincoln Riscoff pretty much included the word *shouldn't*, but it hadn't stopped me yet.

I lowered the squeegee into the bucket and turned to the woman. "Is there a restroom I can use?"

She looked up from her task. "Staff restrooms are next to the kitchen, the basement, or out in the garage. Don't even think about using another one, or Mrs. Riscoff will toss you out of this house on your ear."

If she knew what I was doing with her son, she'd do even more than that, I'm sure.

I couldn't even believe she let Gables into the house to clean. Then again, when I brought that up, it sounded like Jackie's friend didn't mention our last name to the head housekeeper when she hired us.

"Got it. I'll be back then."

"Try not to get lost. I spent my whole first month here wandering around like an idiot, and nearly got fired."

I nodded with a polite smile affixed to my face and left the room.

My heart pounded and my palms sweated as my sneakers squeaked on the marble floor. For some insane reason, the scene from *Pride and Prejudice* where Elizabeth was walking through Pemberley on a tour came to mind. Was this how she felt? Like she knew she shouldn't be there? Probably, but then again, Elizabeth was also thinking, *Of all this, I might have been mistress.* Her version of mistress and mine were totally different.

There was no way I would ever rule over this estate. I glanced out at the gorge through the wall of windows I passed.

Nope. This isn't for me. The Riscoffs probably kept their mistresses hidden far away from the wives.

Oh my God. Why would I even think that? I wasn't going to be anyone's kept woman. Ever. And Lincoln and I couldn't be together openly, so why was I even tiptoeing toward the grand staircase to meet him?

Because I'm dick-struck. That was all. It was good sex. Great sex. I was hooked on what he could do in bed. I nodded my head like I was agreeing with myself when I knew it was all bullshit. I was getting in too deep. I felt things I shouldn't feel.

I crept up the staircase, checking over my shoulder every other step, waiting for someone to question my presence and throw me out of the house.

I'm sorry. I got lost. That was the best excuse I'd have. It worked for their real staff, right?

As soon as I reached the second floor, a voice echoed down the hall to the left.

Shit. I bolted up the next flight, and my heart was hammering by the time I hit the landing. I barely had a chance to catch my breath before someone grabbed my wrist.

I stifled my scream with my free hand.

"I didn't think you would come."

I stared at Lincoln's perfect face and questioned every single decision I'd made for the last month.

He was the heir to this grand estate. I was the help, at least for today. This couldn't be more cliché if we'd tried.

"I can't do this."

His gaze intensified. "Stop."

I held up my hand to silence him when the treads on the stairs creaked. "Someone's coming," I whispered.

Lincoln wove his fingers into mine and pulled me down the hallway to the right. There were so many doors, but he knew exactly where he was going. He pushed open the fifth on the left and shut it behind us.

"Didn't you hear me? I said I can't do this. Not here. We're *in your parents' house.*"

His lips skimmed my collarbone. "Technically, it's my grandfather's house."

"Minor detail. Also, I'm *working.*"

He pressed a kiss on my hammering pulse. "No, you're on a break because I haven't gotten to see you in a week and I've fucking missed you. What were you doing that had you so busy?"

He missed me. I hated that I loved hearing those words so much, but I couldn't deny the tendrils of warmth snaking through me.

"Working. Saving up money. That's what normal people do."

"There's nothing normal about you." Before I could sputter an outraged retort, he continued. "You're extraordinary. Incredible. The most amazing woman I've ever met."

"You just want to get laid." I rolled my eyes, even as I soaked up the compliments.

Lincoln pulled away and his hazel gaze intensified. "That's not what this is about."

I tilted my head to the left. "Really? So if I told you we weren't having sex anymore, you'd be totally okay with it?"

"No. But it's not *just* about the sex. It's you and me and the fact that spending time with you is the best part of my day, week, month, and fucking year. You make me smile and laugh and enjoy life. I didn't want to come back to Gable. I didn't want to make a life here. But you changed that."

Sometimes I hated that he was so sweet, and that the things he said turned my barriers to rubble before I could reinforce them. Whatever argument I was planning to make faded away as I ran my fingers through his dark hair and tugged his mouth to mine.

"Just kiss me. I missed you too."

His eyes lit up at my admission. It was the first time I'd said anything like that.

"Fucking finally."

His lips crashed against mine, and I got lost in the kiss. I twined one leg around his hip and pressed against him. My nipples peaked against my bra, and I wanted him.

Even though I told myself how much I hated the forbidden aspect of our meetings, there was something about it that was undeniably hot. The thought of getting caught terrified me, but it also increased the urgency a thousand times over.

Lincoln's palm slid along my hip and beneath my cut-off shorts. "Fuck. No panties today?"

My cheeks heated with embarrassment because now I had to admit that I wanted him to touch me like this in his parents' house. That I wanted this to happen. That it couldn't fit into my dirty fantasies about him more perfectly than if I'd planned it myself.

As his fingers skimmed my wet lips, he groaned. "Fuck me. I was just going to tease you. Get you as worked up as I am, and then meet you tonight. But there's no fucking way I'm letting you leave this room without sinking my cock into this little wet pussy."

It was on the tip of my tongue to say *we can't*, but the words wouldn't come.

"We have to hurry," I said instead.

Lincoln lifted me off my feet and carried me across the room. I was too busy working my lips across his chiseled jawline to do more than notice the masculine interior of the room.

"I've wanted you in my bed since that first night. I've never been with anyone here."

I lifted my eyes to his face. "Ever?"

"Never. Only you. And it feels so fucking right."

He pressed me against the bed, and even though I knew this was a terrible idea, I couldn't help but agree—it felt so right.

"Hurry. We have to hurry. I need you."

Lincoln bowed to my demands and quickly stripped and donned the condom as I tugged off my shorts. He nudged my knees wider apart and slid the head of his cock along my wetness.

"You still have to meet me tonight. I want to go slow. Take my time. I hate rushing with you. You deserve better."

At that moment, I'd say anything he wanted to hear, and promising to meet him again was no hardship.

"Yes."

He pushed inside, and my body stretched to accommodate his size. I kept expecting the next time to be less incredible than the last, but somehow it never was. It was like Lincoln was on a mission to keep me addicted to him, and he was winning on every level.

When he thumbed my clit, I bit down on his shoulder to muffle my instinctive scream. My biting didn't turn him off, though. It had the opposite effect. He turned wild, fucking into me like a man possessed. My orgasm crashed into me, and my body clamped down hard on him. When Lincoln came, he didn't muffle his yell. The roar filled the room, and I froze beneath him.

Oh. Fuck.

"Lincoln!" I whisper-yelled his name. "Someone had to hear that."

"Fuck," he said under his breath and dropped his forehead against mine. "I'm tired of hiding, Blue. Tired of sneaking around. I wish we could just—"

I kissed him to silence his words. "We don't have a choice."

He lifted his head again. "We always have a choice. Sometimes I wish we'd get caught and that would take the decision out of both our hands."

"Don't you dare say—"

"Lincoln? Are you okay?" a woman said from outside the door as she knocked. "I heard you yell."

"Please tell me you locked the—"

Before I could finish my plea, the door burst open and she stepped inside. Her eyes locked onto mine and recognition hit her face in less than a second. Mine followed a moment later.

Mrs. Riscoff.

"Lincoln Bates Roosevelt Riscoff, what is she —I can't—"

Lincoln grabbed the comforter and threw it over us. "Mother, leave now."

"That Gable whore's daughter? You can't possibly be—"

"Mother, I suggest you don't say another word. Whitney is my—"

Mrs. Riscoff's face paled before she made a choking sound and groaned. She stumbled two steps backward before clutching her arm and then her chest.

"Help," she mumbled before she fell against the wall and slid down until she hit the floor.

"Fuck. Fuck. Fuck."

Lincoln levered off me and whipped on his pants before rushing to his mother's side.

"Mother. Mother. Hang on." He turned back to me. "Call 911."

WHITNEY

Present day

Sweet Jesus. Not again.

Gabi's eye-shadow palette clatters to the floor as I jump out of the chair and rush to the hallway, my robe flapping open. I yank it shut as I slide to a stop next to McKinley Riscoff, who is on her knees beside her mother.

"Call 911!" She says it again, this time to a passing worker who pulls out her cell phone to dial. "Mother, please stay with me."

"Oh God. This is bad," Gabi whispers from behind me, and she's absolutely right.

I have to get the hell out of here. Last time, I was certain Mrs. Riscoff was faking it, and I was wrong.

"Get her out of here."

Mrs. Riscoff's raspy voice sends shivers down my spine. As much as I don't like this woman, I wouldn't wish death on anyone. All I can do is comply with her wishes and disappear.

I turn and run for the locker room to grab my clothes and

find my aunt. I don't want to be on Riscoff property for one second longer than I have to be.

I knew coming here was a terrible idea.

Aunt Jackie finds me in the locker room before I can go looking for her.

"What's going on? We got the alert for a medical emergency, and one of my housekeepers saw you running in here."

"Mrs. Riscoff. She saw me. She collapsed."

My aunt's face blanches, and I know exactly what she's thinking before she says it.

"Good Lord. Not again."

That day at the Riscoff estate, Jackie, her two other employees, and I were escorted to the gate and kicked off the property without being paid.

It didn't take long for everyone in town to find out what happened. Jackie's cleaning business slowed to almost nothing when word got around about what I'd done. At least, her normal business slowed down. All of a sudden, she was inundated with requests by men to clean houses when their wives were out of town. *Because they all thought her niece wasn't picky about sleeping with clients.*

"Sylvia hardly ever comes here. Ms. Riscoff made that clear, and she hired me anyway. I never thought—"

With shaking hands, I pull on my shorts and slip my shirt over my head. "I shouldn't have come home. This is just another disaster in the making."

"At least she didn't catch you in bed with her son. Seeing that a second time might've actually killed her."

I cringe as I shove my feet into sandals. "Please, don't remind me. I need to get out of here. I . . . I can't stick around to see what happens."

Jackie nods and pulls her car keys out of her pocket. "Go.

I'll catch a ride home with someone. You don't need to come back to pick me up."

I can read between the lines. Jackie doesn't want me coming back here while she's responsible for me. I can't blame her. I never want to come back.

Then I remember Cricket's wedding.

"What am I going to tell Cricket? I can't—"

Jackie shakes her head. "We're not going to worry about that now. Just go. We'll figure it out later."

I take her keys and rush out of the locker room, hoping like hell I don't see anyone else who might recognize me on the way out.

As if I could be so lucky.

LINCOLN

My sister's words repeat in my head as I bolt for the private exit from my office.

"The ambulance is coming. Mother had another episode with her heart. It happened after she saw Whitney Gable in the spa."

It's like the past repeating itself, and part of me wonders if it's real or fake this time. A good son would take the information at face value, but after years of my mother's manipulations, I find it difficult to give her the benefit of the doubt.

Her cardiac episode ten years ago triggered by seeing Whitney and me together was real, according to the family's doctor. This one? Fuck, who knows.

Her hatred of the Gable family will never die.

I reach the parking garage and jump in my Range Rover and haul ass out of the lot, tires squealing, barely waiting for the barrier to open completely. Two minutes later, I reach the resort road and take the back entrance. The sensor in my SUV triggers the gate.

I fly up to the front and slam on the brakes before

throwing it into park and jumping out to head for the employee entrance.

The door flies open and a dark-haired woman rushes out, not looking where she's going. She slams into my chest.

"I'm so sorry—" She looks up, and it's another punch to the gut.

"Whitney."

All the blood drains from her face. "I swear I didn't do anything. I didn't. I—"

My instincts kick into overdrive, and I wrap my arms around her. "Shhh, Blue. You didn't do anything. I know it's not your fault."

Her entire body shakes in my hold. "She hates me so much. I should never have come home."

I squeeze her tighter, and everything about having her in my arms feels so fucking *right*. "It's going to be okay. This isn't your fault."

She lifts her blue eyes to mine, and the sight of tears flooding them guts me. "It doesn't matter where I go. I ruin everything."

I don't know what makes me do it, but I cup her cheek like I used to. "You ruined me, and I don't even fucking care." I lower my mouth to hers as a tear tips over her lid.

When our lips meet, it's like being thrown back ten years into the past. Like there's never been a single moment in time that she hasn't been mine. My need for her is still as strong as ever. She'll never be out of my blood.

Whitney shoves at my chest and tears out of my arms. "Don't. I can't."

She runs for the parking lot, and I remember that my mother is awaiting paramedics.

I'm a shitty son.

Regardless of what happens to my mother, as I watch Whitney run from me again, I vow it'll be the last time.

This isn't over.

WHITNEY

The past

I REFUSED to see Lincoln again, and I barely went out in public anymore. Whenever I did, people stared. Mrs. Riscoff must not have been thinking about the repercussions of cursing my name to anyone who would listen while they loaded her on a stretcher, because now the whole town knew that Lincoln and I had been caught together.

No one would talk about it in front of him, I was sure. They were probably too afraid of what he would do. But no one feared my reaction.

I walked into Freedom Bean to get Aunt Jackie a latte, at her request, even though I begged not to go, and saw my cousin Karma with a group of girls.

At least she's family, so I don't have to worry about her talking shit.

Or so I thought until I put in the order and waited near the other end of the barista station and overheard laughter. I glanced over my shoulder and they all looked away.

"Why would he touch *her*? He could have anyone. I know she's your cousin, but . . . really?"

Karma met my gaze, not even trying to be sly. "Probably because he knew she'd put out. Like mother, like daughter."

My mouth dropped open as her betrayal flayed me in half. *What? Like mother, like daughter?*

I'd been hiding away, avoiding everyone—including my parents—but apparently there was something going on that no one had told me.

I didn't want to do this here, but Karma had given me no choice.

With crossed arms, I stalked over to the table and confronted her. "What the hell are you talking about?"

One of her friends, Jolene, smirked. "You haven't heard? Your mom got caught sneaking out of the Wham Bam Motel last night."

The Wham Bam Motel was what everyone called the Wild Basin Motel on the edge of town.

I tried to school my reactions as Jolene kept talking, but I could feel the heat of embarrassment burning my chest and cheeks.

"Everyone knows . . . well, except who she was with. Definitely not your dad. Doesn't he work third shift right now?"

Any oxygen I could have breathed in got sucked out of the room, and I choked. "What?"

Karma crossed her arms to match my posture. "I figured your mom would've told you. But then, it sounds like there's a lot your mom isn't telling you these days. Like who she's having a fling with."

I fought to draw in a breath. "You're full of shit, Karma. And spreading rumors about your own family? That's low."

"They aren't rumors if they're true," Jolene said with a

139

smirk. "Like you and Lincoln. So, how was he? Because I think I'd like to take him for a spin."

Lincoln had been calling me at least five times every day, but I hadn't answered. I'd given his mother a freaking heart attack. I was pretty sure that was as over as we could get.

"He has better taste than you."

All the girls burst out laughing, including my traitor cousin. "Like you?"

I was reduced to feeling an inch tall, but I kept my shoulders back and stood straight. "Give it a try. See how he reacts to skank." My gaze flicked to Karma. "You're a bitch."

"Better a bitch than a whore," she shot back, and my stomach turned.

"Latte for Jackie," the barista called.

"You better run on back to my mom now," Karma said.

I spun around on my sneaker, retrieved the latte, and got the hell out of the coffee shop.

Next up, get the hell out of this town.

LINCOLN

Present day

SITTING in the emergency room of the Riscoff Memorial Hospital with my mother is the last place I should be thinking about Whitney, but I can't help it.

Fuck. What a mess.

We're waiting on tests to come back, but I can't lie and say I think this episode is legitimate. My mother's conveniently timed heart events are growing to legendary status. The last episode happened right after Commodore turned The Gables over to McKinley. Before that, it was when I mentioned the idea of marrying Monica.

Now she has one when she sees Whitney Gable, and we end up in the emergency room?

Suspicious? Absolutely.

"I guess you should've gotten rid of her as soon as she stepped foot in town." Harrison's comment is a poorly aimed swipe.

"This is her home too."

"We own this town. There's nothing here that the Gables can claim."

"Shut up, Harrison," McKinley chimes in. "This is about Mother, and no one else. Pretend you care."

"I'm her favorite. Of course I care."

He's right. If it were up to our mother, Harrison would inherit everything. McKinley and I don't cater to her like he does.

Dr. Green, our family's doctor for the last two decades, enters the waiting area, and we all stand.

"Is she going to be okay?" my sister asks.

"Was it a heart attack?" That question comes from Harrison.

"She's going to be fine. It was a panic attack. Your mother has been under a lot of stress lately, and it's taking a toll on her."

"So, what can we do to help her, Doc?" Harrison glances pointedly at me.

"Try to avoid introducing additional stressors into her life. She needs some peace and quiet. She's been through a lot over the years."

I scoffed. "She doesn't work. Hasn't worked a day in her life. She has staff at her beck and call to do literally every single thing she could possibly need. How stressful can her life really be?" I may sound heartless, but I'm done with my mother using her health to try to manipulate every situation.

Dr. Green's gaze rests on me. "I think you're well aware of what triggered her panic attack, Mr. Riscoff."

My jaw clenches, and I want to demand a second opinion. My mother obviously has Green wrapped around her finger. He'll tell us whatever she wants him to.

"Can we see her now?" McKinley asks.

"Yes. And she'll be able to leave shortly. I might suggest

having her spend some time out of town. Maybe she could go on a trip and relax?"

"Good luck with that," Harrison says with a cough. "She hates traveling this time of year."

"I suggest you try convincing her then. I'll plan to visit her tomorrow at home to see how she's doing and reassess."

"Thank you, Dr. Green. Will you take me back to her?" McKinley asks before she follows Dr. Green out of the private waiting area.

Harrison turns to me. "If you're trying to kill her, you're doing a hell of a job."

"Fuck off." I stand and turn for the door.

"If she finds out that someone is trying to exhume Dad's body for a paternity suit, that'll really put her over the edge."

I stop short on the threshold. "How did you find out about that?"

Harrison smirks. "I know everything. Now . . . it'll be interesting to see if you find out what it's like to not have a claim to everything you think you deserve, big brother."

WHITNEY

I DON'T KNOW where to go. I don't want to bring the destruction that comes with me back to Aunt Jackie's yet.

Jesus, what if Mrs. Riscoff dies? Aunt Jackie will lose her job for sure.

Not that a job is life and death, but if Jackie were to get fired from The Gables, she'd probably have to move. Like she told me before, the Riscoffs own nearly everything and control the majority of the jobs in this town.

I never should have come home.

And why did I let him kiss me?

The last thing I need in my life is to complicate it by adding Lincoln Riscoff to the fray. I've only been home for a couple of days, and everything is already falling apart.

I don't want to go through this again. The whispers. People talking about me wherever I go. I left Gable to make it stop, and that's the same reason I escaped LA.

It doesn't matter where I go—I'm cursed.

I point the car in the only direction that feels like a viable option. There's only one person I know who would probably hand me an award if Sylvia Riscoff were to die just from seeing me.

My great-uncle Magnus.

HIS CABIN IS MORE of a shack precariously held up on the side of the gorge that leads down to the river. I have no idea how he's able to maneuver the rickety stairs that wind to the water since he doesn't have a fancy hydraulic chair on a rail like the house next door, but the fishing pole on the platform below tells me he's been out there recently.

I knock on the cracked wooden door and am met with the sound of a cocking shotgun.

"Who is it?"

Magnus always was a crotchety old man, and that hasn't changed.

"It's Whitney. Your grand-niece."

After a few thumps, he pulls open the door. "I know who the hell you are. 'Bout damn time you came around to show some respect to your elders."

"I think I might've killed Sylvia Riscoff."

His rheumy blue eyes widen. "'Bout damn time someone did that too." He jerks his bald head toward the inside of the house. "Come on in. I've got some moonshine that'll go nice with this story."

I step inside the cabin and pick my way across the uneven boards. For a man older than dirt, he moves with more pep in his step than I would have expected. In fact, he seems just as nimble as he was ten years ago.

He snags a mason jar off the counter and walks out the slider onto the deck. "Hear your daughter-in-law almost kicked it today, Commodore!"

Good Lord. Commodore Riscoff lives next door?

I don't know when that happened, but that's the worst thing I could imagine for these two. Commodore still lived at the Riscoff estate when I left Gable, but neither he nor Magnus ever miss a chance to rile the other and keep the feud alive.

Like that lit rag Magnus shoved in the gas tank of Commodore's fancy Mercedes right before I left town. The car blew up just like in the movies, according to everyone who saw it. Of course, though, no one *actually* saw Magnus do it, or at least no one would admit it. Regardless, there was no doubt in my mind that it was my great-uncle.

"The fuck you say, Gable?"

I step out onto the deck behind Magnus against my better judgment and immediately fear for my life. The railings are barely attached, and there's nothing else to keep me from tumbling into the rushing water of the river below.

Making sure I'm directly in the middle, I turn to the left. A white-haired old man in a fancy-looking chair sits on a much grander deck holding a shotgun pointed in my direction.

"Oh my God." I duck behind Magnus, and he waves an arm.

"Don't shoot my grand-niece. I'll really kill you for that."

I peek over Magnus's shoulder, and Commodore lowers his gun to his lap.

"You finally kill Sylvia, girl?"

I shake my head and realize his eyesight probably isn't good enough to see me.

"They took her to the hospital. Chest pains. I don't know what happened."

The old man's chest shakes with booming laughter. "It's

always chest pains. Mark my words, she'll die of spite when she's older than me."

I don't know exactly how old Commodore Riscoff is, but I think it's a few years north of Magnus's advanced age.

"Guess I better call for an update." He pierces me with a stare, and I realize I might be wrong about his eyesight. "Stay away from my grandson. You hear me? He's gonna give the family an heir, and there ain't gonna be a drop of Gable blood running through that boy's veins."

As Magnus hollers out a few choice slurs, Commodore wheels himself inside, a dog trotting beside him.

I turn to go back in, but Magnus takes a seat on the deck. "Make sure you don't say anything you don't want that old fucker to hear. He's like a hawk even now."

"Shouldn't we go inside then?"

Magnus shakes his head. "Nah. I don't know how many years I got left, but I'm going to spend as much time outside as I can, enjoying this view."

I glance at the pockmarks in the peeling paint of the siding. "Are those from buckshot?"

Magnus nods with what almost looks like a grin on his face. "We like to keep it interesting around here. Otherwise, we might get so bored there's no reason to live."

I scan him for injuries, noting a few spots scabbing over on his arms. "You don't aim at each other . . . do you?"

With a shrug, he ignores my question. "Tell me about this new hullabaloo you caused." He takes a swig of the moonshine and holds it out to me. "Because it seems to me that's your specialty in life these days."

I almost wave off the offer of the home brew, but it's been a rough day. I clasp the glass jar in both hands and take the smallest swig.

I regret the decision immediately as my mouth catches

fire and it spreads down my throat, all the way to my belly. "Jesus Christ." I cough, and Magnus snatches the jar out of my hand before I spill any.

"Don't tell me you went soft living in that city."

I hack up a lung until the flames in my mouth finally settle down and I'm left with the flavor of gasoline. "How do you drink that?"

Magnus shrugs again and swills enough to knock me unconscious, and all he does is smack his lips at the end like it's delicious. *Maybe he really is crazy?*

"We're not talking about me, kid. I want the play-by-play. I assume you came here for a sympathetic ear, and I'm ready to hear every dirty detail."

I bow my head and pinch the bridge of my nose between my left thumb and forefinger. "I didn't even do anything. All I have to do is exist for her to have a heart attack."

"Which seems more like a *her* problem than a *you* problem, to my senile brain." Magnus takes another sip.

"It could be a Jackie problem if she gets fired because of it."

Magnus's shoulders rise and fall again, which has always been half of his communication. "Jackie will land on her feet. She's smart. She's a Gable."

"In this town, that seems to be a liability now as much as it ever was."

"Maybe to Sylvia Riscoff, but that old bat hates everyone and everything. Why do you care what she thinks of you, anyway? You gave her the biggest fuck-you of all time when you rejected her son in front of God and everyone. One of the most entertaining days of my life, I might add."

Why do I care what Mrs. Riscoff thinks of me? Oh, that's right, *guilt.*

"But—"

Magnus holds up a hand. "I know what you're going to say, but nothing that happened a decade ago was your fault. You weren't involved in that mess, so why do you keep trying to take on the responsibility for it?"

The old man is full of questions I'm not ready to answer today.

"I don't know." I release a long breath. "I've been holding on to it for so long, I don't know how to let go."

"No, you've been running so long, you don't know how to stop. Maybe you oughta give that a try and see what it's like to just *be*."

As he takes another swig of moonshine, I wonder how much he's already had today and whether I should be taking his advice. Then again, he's probably immune to its effects by now.

I stare out over the gorge. *God, I missed this view.* But that doesn't matter.

"Sylvia will never let me *just be* in Gable. She'll run me out of town if it's the last thing she does."

Magnus glances over his shoulder at the house a hundred feet away. "Good thing Sylvia isn't the one whose opinion matters in that family."

"Like Commodore would ever take the side of a Gable. You two *shoot at each other*."

"On the daily. Keeps us both on our toes. But he's got a leash on Sylvia, or should I say a tight grip on the purse strings."

I don't quite take his point. "What are you suggesting I do exactly?"

"Put some steel in your spine, hold your ground, and don't let Sylvia Riscoff decide your future." He tilts his head to the right, his gaze sharp. "You never know what might happen."

LINCOLN

MY BROTHER'S words follow me out of the hospital as I watch my sister direct her driver to lift Mother into her SUV to take her home.

"It'll be interesting to see if you find out what it's like to not have a claim to everything you think you deserve, big brother."

His words stay with me as I drive back to my office, and they're still on my mind when my phone rings. *Commodore.*

"I find out from Magnus fucking Gable that Sylvia's having another one of her *episodes*?"

"How did Magnus know?"

"How do you think? That black-haired Gable girl is in his shack right now, probably plotting how to bring about the downfall of the Riscoff clan by leading you around by the balls."

"Whitney's there? With him?" I reach out a hand to brace on the window. "That fucking shack isn't even safe. If that thing falls off the side of the mountain with her in it—"

"Boy, you heard what I said about her. She's bad news.

150

Although, if she accidentally killed your mother, I wouldn't exactly hold it against her."

There has never been any love lost between my grandfather and my mother. She was his pick for my father's wife due to her connections and family, but she apparently hid her true nature until after the wedding. Then everything changed. At least, that's the story Commodore tells. I have a feeling it's a lot more complicated than that. My father never hid the fact that he wasn't happy in his marriage, but he did hide everything else. Or at least, he tried to.

"I'd appreciate it if you wouldn't say that about my mother, sir."

"I know what she is. Sylvia and I agree on one thing and one thing only—no Gables are the best Gables."

I ignore his comment. "Did you tell Harrison about the paternity claim and possible exhumation of the body? Because he knows."

The call silences for a few beats. "I told two people. You and my lawyer. I've been wondering if that boy has informants, and I think we just got our answer."

Fuck. Commodore's lawyer is one of Harrison's sources of information.

"What are we going to do about it? Mother can't find out. It actually might kill her."

"Even better reason to let it go public."

"Commodore." My tone is harsh.

"Fine. I don't want this shit public any more than you do. I'll have to come up with a response that puts them off a while longer, but it won't make it go away. And now I have to fire my goddamned lawyer."

"Offer them a settlement."

"Never." The old man's tone is adamant.

"Why?"

151

"Because that'll invite every other bastard of your father's to come for a piece of the action. If you'd just get down to producing the next generation, we wouldn't even have to worry about this problem."

"And if I don't and the heir is real and older than me? You're really going to consider handing this company over to someone who knows nothing about it?"

"I'll do what I think is right."

"What about protecting and preserving the legacy?"

Commodore doesn't reply to that, and instead changes the subject. "That Gable girl looks like she might be leaving. Not that I should be telling you. Hope she didn't drink any of Magnus's 'shine. She might not make it down the mountain alive."

Fuck.

I hang up the phone, not waiting to hear another word out of his mouth.

LINCOLN

The past

MY MOTHER WALKING in on Whitney and me was basically my worst nightmare, and yet I'd taken the risk all the same. It had been a calculated one, but I'd calculated wrong. Since then, Whitney had refused to see me. I'd tried calling over and over again. The only thing I could do was track her down, because from what I was told, she rarely went out in public anymore.

Because of me. Because I'm a fucking asshole. I had to make this right. I wouldn't be able to live with myself if I didn't.

Which meant going to her house. Whitney hadn't left me any other options, and I was done waiting. I wasn't going to let this be the end.

Who cared if my mother didn't approve? When had I ever let that impact my life choices? I was my own man. I was a fucking Riscoff. We didn't follow orders; we gave them.

I climbed into my truck and turned in the direction of the

bridge nearest Whitney's parents' house instead of the one that led into town.

When I hit the railroad tracks, I took a left and followed the streets to the little house that Whitney's dad bought after they were evicted from their family farm by the sheriff. The farm that Commodore bought at auction, and the house and barn burned down the next day. I doubted we'd ever find out the truth of what happened on that subject.

When I turned in to the driveway, I had no idea whether she was home. Whitney didn't have a car. She borrowed her mom's on occasion, and sometimes her aunt's. Most of the time, she walked or rode her bike.

The one time I mentioned getting her a car, I almost blew my chance to see her ever again. Another thing I miscalculated badly. Pride was one thing my girl had in spades.

Although, based on her behavior, she no longer wanted to be my girl.

Which meant today might end with us being over, once and for all.

Just letting that thought enter my head was like a punch to the gut. It almost doubled me over. *But if she doesn't feel the way I do about her . . .* Was there a point to any of this?

I parked, and the front door flew open as soon as I was out of the truck. Whitney's father stepped out onto the crumbling concrete stoop. "You turn around and go right back the way you came, Riscoff. Your kind ain't welcome here."

"Mr. Gable—"

He pulled a shotgun out from behind the door. "Don't make me shoot you, boy. Because I got no problem getting rid of a body. Especially a Riscoff's."

I slid back into my truck slowly, wanting to say something else. Maybe ask him to tell Whitney I came. Ask him where she was. But there was no way he'd tell me anyway. He'd just as soon kill me.

I gave him a nod and put the truck in reverse. I checked the rearview mirror before I pulled out into the road, and slammed on the brakes.

Whitney stood in the street behind my truck wearing a tank top, cutoffs, and sneakers. Her black hair blew in the wind, and her blue eyes were filled with tears.

The tears slayed me. I slammed the truck into park and ripped open the door. "Blue. Please."

"You get your ass inside, girl." Her father cocked the shotgun.

Whitney squeezed her eyes shut, and a tear streaked down her cheek.

"Just come with me. Please."

Her expression, so torn, it shred me to pieces.

"We can fix this. I promise."

Whitney's lips pressed together.

"Get your ass inside, girl. Don't make me tell you again."

Whitney whipped her head toward her dad as he stomped toward us, shotgun in hand. He was only thirty feet away and closing. I had no idea what he'd do to her when I left.

That thought and the potential answers made my decision for me.

"I'm not leaving you here with him. No way in hell." I held out my hand. "All you have to do is put your hand in mine."

"Don't you fucking dare, girl. I will beat you—"

"Not on my watch." I stepped between Mr. Gable and Whitney. "You'll have to shoot me first."

He lifted the shotgun. "That can be arranged."

Whitney's fingers slid against mine. "Hurry."

I grabbed her hand and we jumped in the truck before he started shooting.

WHITNEY

Present day

ALL I WANT to do is pretend like this day never happened. Rewind. Undo.

But that's not how life works. If I could do that, I'd be living like *Groundhog Day*, because my life has been one big mess of bad decisions. And most of them can be traced right back to Lincoln Riscoff.

Why is it that we can't stay away from each other when we know it always ends badly? And this time I didn't even have to be near him to unleash chaos.

Regardless of how horrible his mother is, I hope she's okay. I hope her "episode" was a ploy to manipulate Lincoln, and that I didn't actually cause her to have a heart attack.

I park Jackie's car in the driveway and walk around the house to the gate in the backyard. I can't stomach the thought of dealing with Karma right now. I've got enough on my mind with Magnus's cryptic words in my head. He thinks I should stay. I don't know how to do anything but run. Where else could I go? Where else would I want to go? My list is filled with a whole lot of blank spaces.

Maybe Magnus is right, and it's time I start making decisions based on what I want rather than what I feel like I'm forced to choose.

I slip inside the backyard gate and walk toward the shed.

"Look what the cat dragged in," Karma drawls with a tone as catty as her comment.

I whip around to see her reclining on a folding lawn chair while her girls play on the swings. "Save it. Please."

"You haven't even been back a week, and you're already the talk of the town—again. That's impressive, even for you."

I look away as she sits up.

"What? Upset you didn't kill the old bat this time?"

"How do you even know that already?" The question bursts from my lips.

"Texts from one of my friends who works at the hospital. Small town. News travels fast."

"Isn't that a legal violation or something?"

Karma rolls her eyes. "Really? That's what you were counting on to stop the gossip? You should've just gone somewhere else. Why the hell did you have to come back here?"

"You know, I've never been able to figure out why you hate me so much."

She crosses her arms over her chest. "Does it matter?"

I reply with a shake of my head. "I guess not. Just . . . leave me alone. Please."

"Then take your freeloading ass somewhere else. If you get Mom fired over this, then we're screwed—and it'll be all your fault. Just like when you got her fired from all her cleaning jobs. Why do you think she doesn't work for herself anymore, Whitney? You think she *wanted* to work for the

Riscoffs? No. She did that because she almost lost the house, and it was her last resort."

Guilt floods my system like poison, crippling me. "I . . . I . . ."

"And then you just ran off and lived it up as a rock star's wife." Karma's tone slices viciously. "Didn't give a single damn about what you left behind. Didn't send a single fucking penny back either. Great family loyalty there, *cuz*."

The bitterness that drips off her tongue is more than I can handle.

"I'll leave then. You'll never fucking see me again. I'll be gone by tomorrow."

"And break Cricket's heart? As if we could get so lucky." Karma pushes off the lounger and waves at her kids. "Come on, girls. Time to go inside."

LINCOLN

"THANKS, MAN. I OWE YOU," I tell Hunter, thankful he answered the phone as quickly as he did. As soon as I made sure my mother was situated at the estate, I knew it was time to find Whitney.

"You sure as hell will owe me if she goes running off again and my bride-to-be loses her maid of honor."

"I won't let that happen."

"The way things have gone between you and Whitney, you need to treat this situation like a case of dynamite. Fucking delicately. The girl has been through hell. According to Cricket, all Whitney wanted to do was get out of LA and find a place to live a quiet life. Out of the public eye. Her life turned real bad after Rango died, and from the sound of it, wasn't much better when he was alive."

"What did he do to her? What did Cricket tell you?"

I never read or listened to anything that had to do with Ricky Rango, but maybe I should have.

"Cricket doesn't share much, but Rango's last message to his fans was that his wife betrayed him and was trying to destroy his career. He said she broke him creatively, and he didn't know if he'd ever be able to write music again. Then he OD'd, and everyone said she pushed him to it. They turned on her. Went completely rabid."

I remember her black eye, and it makes sense now. "Jesus Christ. What a dumb fuck." It lines up with everything I thought about Ricky Rango before. "Selfish little prick."

"You can say that again. And it sounds like she doesn't know anything different. Might want to take that into consideration when you see her."

"Hunt, are you trying to give me relationship advice?"

He coughs. "At this point, I think it's just advice, because you two don't have a relationship."

"*Yet.* I'm working on it. I'm not going to let her run. Not when everyone she needs is right here in Gable."

"Then maybe you should show her what it's like when someone actually gives a damn about her and what she wants. I hear the ladies like that."

I think about how Hunter and Cricket, the perfect example of opposites attract, ended up together. "I can tell you want to say something else, so you might as well just spit it out, Hunt."

"This is the one time in your life when being Lincoln Riscoff might actually hurt your chances of getting what you want."

"You think I don't know that? She made that clear ten years ago."

"I think you need to consider how the hell to turn it to your advantage. Show her what it's like to matter to someone. Show her you can put her first the way Rango never did. She must've seen something in you before. You're not that big of a prick that it's completely gone by now. Show her that again."

I remember that night in the bar, and how shocked

Whitney was to have someone stand up for her. To fight for her.

Hunter's right. This has to be about *her*. It's not about me and my fucked-up family.

"Thanks, man."

"Good luck."

I hang up with Hunter and drive toward Whitney's aunt's house, relieved that I won't have to knock on the front door. Thanks to Hunter, I now know she's living in a shed out back.

She deserves a palace. Not a shed.

Hunter had more than one valid point, but the most important one was that Whitney Gable hasn't been treated right by any man in her life. *Including me.* It's time to change that. And this time, I'm not going to fuck it up.

I'm older. Arguably wiser. I finally understand the value of a good woman in a way I didn't before. Even more, I realize that I was right to think Whitney was special then. She's unlike any woman before or since.

I park my Range Rover in the alley behind the house and spot the peaked roof of the shed in the back corner.

Hoping Hunter was right, I open the gate and close it behind me. There's only one window in the back of the shed, and it's frosted.

Or steamed up?

The sound of water running comes through the thin walls of the shed, and I see movement inside. I'm not about to spy on Whitney if she's in the shower, but then something presses against the glass. A palm. It squeezes into a fist, and another one joins it.

The only thing I can picture is Whitney's head hanging, her hair dripping wet as she sobs in the shower, and the vision guts me just like her tears did ten years ago.

Except last time, she cried in my arms.

LINCOLN

The past

"I ALMOST KILLED YOUR MOM." Whitney's voice broke as I tucked her head under my chin. We were holed up in my truck out in the woods, far from where anyone would ever find us.

"You didn't. It was my fault. I shouldn't have pushed it."

"But I went along with it."

I wiped away the tears that spilled over her lids. "Please, Blue. Stop crying. I can't stand it."

"I can't help it. I have to get out of here. This town. It's . . . I can't stay."

Even though I didn't say it, we both knew I couldn't go. Not if I wanted to take my place at the head of the Riscoff empire. Gable was where we'd been based for over 170 years, and this was where my family would always reign.

"We'll figure something out."

She shook her head. "There's nothing to figure out. This is impossible. We tried. We failed."

I held her tighter because I refused to let her go. I refused to quit.

"Do you love me?" I wasn't going to ask the question. I didn't want to hear the answer if it was no, but I'd run out of time. I had to know.

Whitney turned her face toward the window instead of toward me. My heart clenched in my chest, like it was preparing to be shredded.

"Look at me, Blue. Look me in the eye and tell me you don't love me."

With tears streaming down her face, she lifted her gaze to mine.

Fuck. Maybe I was wrong. Maybe . . .

Finally, she spoke, her voice hoarse from crying. "I shouldn't love you. It would be so much easier if I didn't."

I pulled her tighter against me and pressed a kiss to her forehead.

"Thank God," I whispered. "Because I fucking love you more than I knew was possible. We'll figure this out. We can make it work."

Even as I said the words, with this beautiful girl in my arms, I wondered if I was lying about that last part.

WHITNEY

Present day

SOMEONE KNOCKS on the door of the cabin, and I snuffle back my tears in the shower.

Fucking Karma. She just can't leave me be.

"I already know you want me to leave! I get it. You don't have to tell me again!"

The door opens, and I curse the fact that it doesn't have a lock. I shut the water off and grab for my towel . . . which I left on the futon. I poke my head around the shower curtain, expecting to see my cousin's gloating face. But I'm absolutely and completely wrong.

"That's not what I want. Not at all."

Lincoln.

The shock of seeing him standing there sends a jolt through my system. I stumble backward and my feet slide out from under me. I grab the shower curtain, and it tears off the clips as I fall. Before I hit the floor, strong arms wrap around my body.

"I got you, Blue."

For the space of two heartbeats, I can't make myself struggle free. Just hearing my nickname on his lips again brings back more memories than I can handle. I forgot what it's like to be this close to him. The kiss earlier wasn't enough.

The kiss that happened after I gave his mother a heart attack.

I stumble out of his arms, the shower curtain wrapped around me. "What are you doing here?" It comes out as a demand.

"Where else would I go?"

"To your family. Your mother. Is she . . ." I brace for the answer, expecting the worst.

"She's fine. Panic attack."

I release a pent-up breath. "Thank God."

"I'm more worried about you right now."

I stare into Lincoln's eyes, trying to decide if this is just another game and what his angle is. "I'm fine. I don't need you worrying about me."

He nods, and I try to think of all the things I've waited years to say to him. I try to picture all the ways I've imagined this moment, just like I imagined coming back to Gable in high style and making everyone regret how they mistreated me and my family. But my mind goes blank because all I can think about is how good it felt to have someone stronger than me catch me when I fall.

How pathetic is that?

Tears burn the back of my eyes, and it's a losing battle. I can't stop them from falling.

I tuck my chin to my chest and let them fall. But my silent tears don't escape his notice.

"It guts me to see you cry."

"Then leave." I sniffle as I give the order.

"That's not gonna happen. Not this time."

LINCOLN

I STEP CLOSER. When Whitney doesn't bolt, I wipe her tears away, just like I've done before, but everything is different this time. I fucking swear it will be.

As my thumb sweeps along her cheekbone, Whitney flinches. I tuck her hair behind her ear and look closer. The greenish purple is unmistakably a fading bruise. Instantly, rage grips me.

"Who the fuck hit you?"

Whitney jerks her head back, letting her hair fall forward to cover it again. "It doesn't matter."

"Everything about you matters to me. I don't think you get that."

Whitney looks up, her eyes still shiny from the tears. "Is that your new game? Make me feel like I'm worth something to you now?" She looks away, and I hate that she thinks it's a ploy.

"You've always been worth your weight in gold, Whitney." I say her name because I know it'll get her attention. "Now, tell me who hit you."

Her chin juts out, and I recognize the stubbornness I remember.

"It's been taken care of."

"If he's not six feet under, he hasn't been taken care of. No man hits a woman. Give me a name."

"I handled it. I'm a big girl now. I take care of my business. I don't need you or your money. You still can't buy me, Lincoln."

I remember the last time she told me that, and it hits hard. "You're right. Because you were fucking priceless then, and I didn't realize it until it was too late."

Whitney looks away, and I hope it's because she doesn't want me to see how the truth affects her.

"I'm not having this conversation. Not now. Not ever. We can't go back. We can't change the past. It's time to move on." She charges for the futon, but the shower curtain is stuck under my foot, and stays stuck.

The pink material shreds, and Whitney's mouth drops open. She wraps her arms around herself and rushes toward her towel, but not before I see every curve of her body.

Fucking Christ.

Whitney Gable is even more devastating now than she was ten years ago. Rounder hips. Fuller tits. Every single inch is perfection.

The dumbest thing I ever did was give her a reason to walk away from me and marry Ricky Rango.

I may not be able to change the past, but I can sure as hell make sure it doesn't repeat itself.

WHITNEY

The past

"I can't believe I let you talk me into this. Everyone's staring." I whispered the words, sure Lincoln could barely hear me over the gasps coming from around us.

"Ignore them. Act like they don't exist."

That was easy for him to say. Lincoln had probably never felt out of place in his life. He walked into Table like he owned it.

Oh, wait, he did. Or at least, his family did. It was the fanciest restaurant in town and located in The Gables.

I must have been insane to say yes.

I tugged my best dress down further to cover more of my thighs. I hadn't realized it was a little shorter than the last time I wore it—to my senior prom that Ricky had come home for and stayed two hours before he left.

I hadn't told Lincoln yet, but Ricky kept calling and texting. He even sent me a freaking handwritten letter with a love song he wrote. But Ricky's a half-assed songwriter at his best, and I couldn't stop myself from fixing the chorus, bridge, and two and a half of the three verses before sending it back to him.

He'd probably record it and make a boatload of money. Just like he did of the single that was currently on the radio. A single that no one knew I wrote the lyrics.

A waiter in a black suit and white shirt arrived at our table. "What can I get for you this evening, sir?"

Lincoln rattled off the name of a wine I'd never heard of, which wasn't surprising because I only drank the kind of wine that came in bottles with twist-off caps and tasted like fruit punch. The man gave him a nod and walked away.

"The steak is great. The fish is fresh. You really can't go wrong with any of it."

My entire body vibrated with the urge to bolt. "I don't belong here. We should be at Cocko Taco or Sub Shack."

My fingers trembled as I reached for my glass of water, and Lincoln clasped my hand before I could reach it.

"You're better than that."

And that was where he was wrong. I wasn't better than that. There was nothing wrong with those places. They just weren't expensive and fancy, part of a world where I'd never be comfortable.

But I couldn't tell Lincoln that. Especially not right here, right now. From the corner of my eye, I could see a woman wearing more diamonds around her neck than I'd ever seen in my life. Her face was twisted into an expression that looked like she smelled something rotten.

Before I could think of anything to say, the man returned with the bottle of wine. He and Lincoln went through some fancy sniffing-and-tasting song and dance that seemed absolutely ridiculous.

When the man poured a measure into my glass, I stared at it like it was a foreign object. "I'm sure it's fine. Thanks."

He gave me a silent nod and left us again.

"I don't know anything about wine," I blurted.

"And you think I care about things like that?"

"I'm going to embarrass you." I looked at all the silverware lined up around my plate. "I don't know what half of these are for. I'm used to one knife, fork, and spoon. I can't—" Before I could finish, another man stepped up to the table, and I shut my mouth so quickly that my teeth clacked together.

"Mr. Riscoff, it's a pleasure to have you dine with us this evening, sir. The kitchen has been informed of your arrival, and all your favorite off-menu dishes are being prepped in case you would like one." He looked at me. "And welcome to you, Ms. . . ."

"Gable. Whitney Gable." When Lincoln gave him my name, it seemed like the entire restaurant hushed as he said it, and now my name echoed throughout the giant gilded room.

If everyone in the restaurant weren't watching us before, they sure as hell were now.

The man's dark eyebrows darted up toward his receding hairline and he cleared his throat. "Welcome, Ms. Gable. I hope Table's cuisine is acceptable to you this evening."

"I'm sure it'll be like a dream," I said, reaching for my wine.

Apparently, the dream was a terrible one, because I missed and knocked the glass over. As red wine stained the snowy white tablecloth, I jumped out of my seat.

"Oh my God, I'm so sorry." I dabbed at it with my napkin, cringing.

"Blue. Stop. It's okay. They'll get us a new one. Just sit down."

Lincoln's smile looked genuine, but my cheeks burned with embarrassment. This was an absolute disaster.

"I need to use the ladies' room. Excuse me."

I rushed away from the table without looking for the facilities. Instead, I headed straight for the entrance.

"I can't do this. I can't do this." I repeated it to myself over and over as I walked blindly into the hotel, my only goal to find somewhere to hide.

When I spotted a row of alcoves that looked like they were for people to make private phone calls, I ducked inside one. Wrapping my arms around my waist, I took several deep breaths, trying not to cry as I rocked back and forth on my cheap heels. I couldn't even look at Lincoln's face before I ran away. I was sure he was regretting his decision to bring me here tonight.

Why, of all places, would he think this was a good idea for the first time we went out together in public? What about starting small?

Then again, it probably didn't occur to him to go anywhere but the best place in town. He was probably trying to impress me. Little did he realize, I would have been happier with a picnic in the maze where no one would bother us and we wouldn't have to worry about prying eyes and whispered words.

"Where do you think you're going?"

A man's sharp voice interrupted my thoughts, and for a moment I thought he was talking to me. I glanced around the corner and saw him grab a woman's arm.

To my horror, it wasn't just any man or any woman. It was Roosevelt and Sylvia Riscoff, Lincoln's parents.

Mrs. Riscoff attempted to tug free of her husband's grip. "To stop this insanity! Our son is at Table with that Gable whore, and I will not stand for it."

"And how are you going to handle it? By causing a public scene? Come with me."

I turned my head and let my hair hang over my face as he pulled her into the alcove beside mine.

Can this night get any worse? As soon as the question popped into my mind, I knew the answer was most definitely *yes.*

"I refuse to let him humiliate us like that."

"If you think confronting him with her is going to do anything but push him further away from the path you want him to take, you're crazy, Sylvia."

"But—"

"He's young. He's pissed that my father called him home from being out in the world and fucking everything that moves. Now he's stuck in Gable for the rest of his life. Don't you realize this is his way of rebelling? He might be a man, but he's a Riscoff. He doesn't like taking orders. Stop treating him like a child and let him have his fling."

"And what if he's serious about this girl? What if it's more?"

Roosevelt choked out a laugh, but there was no humor in it for me.

"Don't be ridiculous. The boy isn't stupid. She's forbidden. A conquest. This fascination of his will burn itself out before you know it—unless you keep causing scenes that make him want to hold on tighter. Let the boy have his little whore for now. He'll get it out of his system and be ready to settle down."

"If he gets her pregnant—"

"It'll be taken care of. Commodore would never let that happen. I'll talk to him tomorrow. If Lincoln insists on challenging his decision, my father will make it clear that Lincoln's status as heir apparent, after me, will disappear. He'll fall into line. *If* you leave him alone."

I could practically feel the hatred pouring off Mrs. Riscoff when she spoke next.

"And in the meantime, you just want me to let him humiliate us? Drag the family name through the dirt by flaunting that Gable girl?"

Roosevelt's voice turned droll. "Don't worry. He'll learn to hide it better as he gets older."

Mrs. Riscoff's sharp inhale preceded a slap, and her heels clicked off even faster than they'd arrived.

I was trying not to throw up in this little alcove and wondering where the nearest exit was when Lincoln's father's footsteps clipped on the marble floor—and stopped right in front of me.

"Did you hear all that, girl?"

I looked up and froze. Roosevelt stared directly at me with a smirk on his face that had none of the charm of Lincoln's. Any response I might be able to come up with was stuck behind the lump in my throat.

"Don't get any notions of reaching above your station. It's never worked for any of the women in your family, and it won't work for you." He tilted his head to the side. "But at least my son has good taste."

His gaze raked over my body, stopping on my bare legs, and I felt filthy.

"Staff entrance is around back. Tell one of the drivers I gave orders to take you home. If you walk back into that restaurant tonight, I'll make sure you regret it."

With a smug smile, he walked off, and I was left reeling.

One thing I knew for sure. I wasn't going back in.

WHITNEY

"YOU JUST LEFT ME THERE. Alone. Waiting for you to come back. For half a fucking hour. If you were worried about people talking about us before, you picked an even better way to make sure they had juicier gossip to talk about."

My lips stayed locked together as I listened to Lincoln lecture me as he paced the cabin. I had no idea why I even came. I'd been planning on telling him everything I over-heard and about the threat his dad made, but something stopped me.

Maybe Lincoln really was just with me as a rebellion. If he knew his parents were letting him "get me out of his system," it would make him even more stubborn about staying with me. *And that's not real.* I didn't want to get caught up in a Riscoff family power struggle where I had no business being.

"You shouldn't have taken me there to begin with. I don't know what you were trying to prove, but it didn't work."

"I was trying to prove that I care about you, and I don't give a damn what anyone else thinks."

I nodded, holding back tears. "Are you sure? Because it

felt like you were trying to rub it in your family's face that you don't give a damn what *they* think."

He turned toward me. "So what if I am? Isn't that what you want me to do? Pick you over them?"

"No! I don't want any part in your family's battles. I don't want to wonder if you only want me because I'm the girl you're not supposed to have." I spun around and headed for the door, but Lincoln gripped my hand before I could touch the handle.

"I wanted you from the very first fucking second I saw you. I didn't know your name. Didn't give a damn who you were. I still don't. That's what I'm trying to show you." His breath brushed my ear, and my entire body heated instantly. "Just let me show you, Blue."

His tone was so soft and tempting, I melted against his chest.

"I don't know how to do this. It's too much," I whispered.

He turned me around in his arms and buried his hand in my hair. "Then fuck everything else and just be with me tonight. I need you."

He pressed the bulge in his pants against me, and I knew it was pointless to pretend I didn't need him too.

Just one last time.

"I need you more."

WHITNEY

Present day

Lincoln's gaze leaves trails of heat down my back as I go snatch up my towel. I know I look different than I did at twenty-one, but that's the least of my worries right now.

My biggest concern? How easily my body responds to his presence. The fact that my nipples are hard has nothing to do with the cool air in the shed, and everything to do with the fact that he was the best I've ever had—which isn't something I'll ever admit.

I wrap the scratchy towel around me before spinning to face him.

Except he's not where I left him. He's right here. Only a foot away. He moved so silently, I didn't have any warning.

And the intensity blazing in those hazel eyes is the kind that has haunted me for a decade.

"You're so fucking beautiful."

I swallow, tugging the towel tighter. "You should go."

"Not before we—"

I have no idea what was going to come out of his mouth because Karma's voice interrupts.

"Wow. Didn't know you were going for a blast-from-the-past fuck, cuz."

"Karma—"

"What? If you're okay with being a Riscoff's whore after everything that happened, you should be able to handle the talk about it. This should be fun."

"Call her a whore again and I'll make you regret it." Lincoln's threat slices out like a whip, and Karma's lips pinch together.

"You Riscoffs think you're so high-and-mighty—"

"Go away, Karma. Whatever you want, I'll deal with you later."

She turns her venom on me once more. "My mom's home. I just wanted to let you know she's unemployed. Good job, Whit. Way to come home and fuck everything up."

Karma salutes and backs out of the shed, leaving Lincoln and me staring after her light brown hair flopping over her shoulder.

Aunt Jackie lost her job? Oh God. I have to fix this.

"Your cousin's a bitch," Lincoln says as the door snaps shut.

With a shake of my head, I sink onto the futon, devastated at what I've wrought.

"I thought your sister wouldn't fire her over this." I shake my head as I try to wrap my brain around what happened today. "I never should've come home. It was a mistake. I need to leave before I ruin anything else."

Lincoln crouches in front of me. "Don't say that. I'll talk to McKinley. There's gotta be something going on. She was with my mom. McKinley wouldn't have had time to fire anyone, plus, she's not spiteful like that. You might not believe it, but some Riscoffs are good people. She's one of them."

"Aunt Jackie needed that job. I have to fix this."

"Let me worry about it. I can fix it. All you have to do is promise you won't skip town before we have a conversation that's long overdue."

Just like a decade ago, my instincts go to war. His hazel gaze urges me to agree, but I know I should stay as far away from Lincoln Riscoff as humanly possible.

"I don't think that's a good idea. There's nothing we need to talk about."

Lincoln's features stay soft, but his stare intensifies. "That's where you're wrong, Blue. There is a hell of a lot that needs to be said. The way things ended—"

"They ended the only way they could have. Maybe that's the way it should stay. It's been a long time, and nothing good has ever come from a Riscoff and a Gable together."

Maybe? Why am I already wavering in my conviction? Because this is Lincoln I'm dealing with, and refusing him anything is a legendary feat.

"I don't know about you, but I remember a lot of good things that came from a Gable and a Riscoff being together."

His deep voice turns rough, and my skin tingles like I'm wishing he would reach out to touch me.

What is wrong with me? Wait, it's not me, it's him. Just being around him sends my body and my mind into a tailspin.

Ten years ago, my addiction to Lincoln Riscoff was dangerous and altered my life in a way I never fully recovered from. Now? It would be even crazier. He's the heir to a billion-dollar empire, and I'm infamous. The stakes are higher. We both have more to lose. He could never give me what I want—a quiet, simple life out of the limelight.

"I can almost hear your brain coming up with reason after

reason not to agree with anything I say, but that doesn't mean I'll stop trying, Blue. There are some mistakes a man only makes once, and losing you was one of them."

I squeeze my eyes shut, not wanting to see the sincere expression on his face. If I'm not careful, he'll do what he always did and convince me against my better judgment.

With a deep breath, I find my fortitude and meet his stare once more. "I was young and dumb, and I made terrible decisions back then that I've paid for over and over again. I'm trying to start fresh, and I can't take the chance of making the same mistakes again. Whatever you think you want from me, you don't. I'm not that girl anymore. I'm older and hopefully a hell of a lot smarter. I think it's best if you go." I'm incredibly proud of myself that my voice doesn't quaver as I deliver my speech.

Lincoln rises. "I'll go, but first, I have to say that you're right—we did make bad decisions. We let other people come between us. You're not the same girl you were back then, and I'm not the same hotheaded kid with something to prove. I've learned too. I know the value of what I lost. You don't know what I want from you, Blue. But you will, when you're ready."

I stand, on the verge of telling him I'll never be ready, but he backs up and grasps the door handle.

"I'll make sure your aunt has a job, and then I'll be back. You and I aren't done. We won't be done until you can tell me that I mean absolutely nothing to you and mean it."

Lincoln pushes the door open and slips out before I have a chance to lie to him.

I flop back on the futon and yank a blanket over my head.

He meant what he said. He'll be back, and before he returns, I need to learn how to say it convincingly.

LINCOLN

I STEP out of the shed, and Jackie Gable stalks toward me from the back patio of the house. Her face is hard as she meets me at the back gate.

"I know what you're thinking. You think if you can get my job back, then you've got a clear shot at my niece. Your plan isn't going to work, though, because I quit." She keeps her voice low, and the challenge in it is impossible to miss.

Stubborn Gable women. They might actually be the death of me.

"Why the hell would you quit? Whitney said you need that job."

"You think I want to be associated with your family after what your mother said to my niece?"

"That's some expensive pride."

She crosses her arms over her chest and her chin goes up. "Damn right, and I'm willing to stand up for it."

"Like my sister stood up for you when she brought you on? Even though my mother demanded she fire you immediately? I remember you being in a tough spot back then."

Jackie's lips flatten. "It's none of your damn business what kind of a spot I was in, then or now."

"It's my business when you leave my sister in the lurch after she went out on a limb for you. I thought you respected her more than that."

Something flits across Jackie's face, telling me I scored a hit.

"Your sister is the only decent one of you. She understands what I had to do. Now, get the hell out of my yard and don't come back. We don't need any more of the kind of trouble you bring. We've got plenty of our own already."

Instinct claws at me to fix this by throwing money at it. To somehow make Jackie Gable not hate me for something I didn't do or say. Or maybe she hates me for not protecting Whitney from my mother. I'm sure there's a plethora of reasons I could choose, but instead, I turn and walk away.

Sometimes, the only thing you can do is retreat, regroup, and work out a new strategy before you end up saying things you can't take back.

LINCOLN

The past

WHITNEY'S PHONE rang quietly on the table over and over while she was in the shower.

I told myself I wasn't going to look. It was none of my business who was calling her. I glanced at the bathroom door, and the water continued to run as the phone rang for the fourth time. If it was her parents and something bad had happened, she'd want to know.

"Your phone's going off," I told her through the door. When she didn't answer, I made an executive decision. It could be an emergency.

I walked to the table and grabbed her phone. Her caller ID read RICKY CALLING.

What the hell? That cheating asshole is still bothering her?

I didn't care that I had to change the radio every time his song came on. He was still a tool, and I could still buy and sell him.

The phone went quiet and immediately started ringing

again.

Anger built up in my chest at the thought of how often he might be harassing her. That shit had to stop. I knew I shouldn't do it, but I answered it anyway.

"You need to stop calling, asshole."

"Who the fuck is this?"

His shocked tone didn't surprise me.

"Whitney's boyfriend."

"The fuck you are!"

"What did you think she was going to do when she found out you cheated on her, you piece of shit? Keep letting you treat her like that? No. She moved on and found a real man."

"Who the fuck is this?" he asked again.

"Lincoln Riscoff."

The call went silent for a moment. "You've gotta be fucking kidding me. She wouldn't touch a Riscoff. Ever. Try again, dick. Better yet, give my girlfriend the phone so I can tell her I got her letter."

Got her letter?

"What the fuck are you talking about?" This time, I was the one shocked.

Ricky laughed like I was the asshole. "My girl still loves me, Riscoff, and she just sent me the proof. If she's with you, it's nothing but a cheap shot at revenge. But don't worry, I'll forgive her. Whitney and I were always meant to be together, and the piece of paper I'm holding proves it."

"Listen to me, you piece of shit—" But Ricky hung up before I could say anything else.

"Who was that?" Whitney came out, towel in one hand, squeezing the water out of her dripping hair.

I didn't care that she was standing four feet away from me, naked. All I heard was Ricky Rango's voice in my head.

185

"My girl still loves me, Riscoff, and she just sent me the proof."

I held out her phone. "You missed a call from your boyfriend."

Confusion creased her features. "What?"

"Ricky Rango called to tell you he got your letter, and he agrees with what you said—that you two are meant to be together." My words came out flat and hollow, which was the exact opposite of how they felt tearing out of my throat.

"What?" she asked, now holding the towel in front of herself.

"Your letter, Whitney. He got it. He forgives you for your revenge fuck."

Her eyebrows climbed toward her hairline as her mouth dropped open. "But—"

"Did you send him a fucking letter?"

"Yes, but—"

She wrote him a letter. She loves him, and I was nothing but revenge. I couldn't fucking believe it, but she didn't deny it.

"I was risking everything to be with you. *Everything.* And you're already making sure your boyfriend is going to take you back after you fuck someone else?" I shook my head, disgust coating every word. "You have thirty seconds to get your clothes and get the fuck out of my sight."

"Lincoln!" Her face was stricken. Probably because her game was up.

I wasn't going to fall for the tears gathering in her blue eyes this time. I hated that I cared that she'd played me. I hated that I gave her the power to rip my heart out like this.

Forcing myself to turn stone cold, I straightened my shoulders and stared at her with dead eyes. *I'm a Riscoff. No one has the power to hurt me. Especially not Whitney Gable.*

I knew that was a lie as soon as I thought it. But apparently I'd gotten really fucking good at lying to myself lately.

"I don't want to hear a fucking word you have to say. Get the hell off my property. I should've never trusted a Gable. I knew better."

WHITNEY

LINCOLN'S WORDS slashed my skin like shards of broken glass, gouging and leaving me shredded. There wasn't a single bit of softness or doubt in his tone. Whatever lies Ricky had told Lincoln about me or us, Lincoln had believed him completely, without even giving me a chance to explain.

I blinked back tears, not wanting him to see them fall after he just threw me away like a piece of trash. I rushed to the bed and grabbed my dress off the floor, then yanked it on.

When I turned around to face him, it was like looking at a stranger. His gaze was filled with hate and disgust. I already knew there was no reasoning with him. And why would I want to defend myself to someone who had already decided I was guilty?

"I don't know what he told you, but you don't know a single fucking thing about anything. You said you loved me." A hysterical laugh bubbled up from my throat. "But you don't have a clue what love is."

Lincoln's mouth twisted cruelly. "Save it, sweetheart. I don't believe a word coming out of your lying mouth. At least it was good for one thing. And that sure as shit wasn't telling the truth."

I sucked in a breath. If he was trying to hurt me and drive me away, he'd scored a direct hit. Tears burned my eyes, but I dashed them away.

"Go fuck yourself. I hope you choke on your own dick."

I ran to the door and grabbed my shoes but didn't bother to put them on. I wasn't standing in this room for another second longer than I had to. When I rushed outside into the pouring rain, there was no chance Lincoln would try to chase me down like the first time I ran from this cabin.

One bad decision after another. *I should have known better.*

Gravel bit into my bare feet as I ran down the driveway toward the road, but I didn't care. I'd rather walk home barefoot, bleeding, and soaking wet than ask Lincoln Riscoff for anything.

Never again.

I was done with men. Done with all of them.

I was almost to the road when headlights cut across my path, and I dodged the front end of an SUV. I tripped on a log and tumbled into the woods. My wrist screamed with pain as I tried to catch my fall.

"Who the hell's there? And what the fuck are you doing on my property?"

I was on my knees, holding my wrist, when someone slammed a door and came around to see me struggling to stand in the mud.

As if this night couldn't get any worse.

Commodore Riscoff.

WHITNEY

Present day

"PLEASE PROMISE me you'll stay. You can't leave, Whit. You just got here." Cricket's begging dumps another million pounds of guilt onto me.

"Your mom quit her job because of me. Don't you think I've done enough damage already?"

"Stop being so melodramatic. Mom's a grown-ass woman. She knew what she was doing when she quit. I'm sure she considered the consequences before she handed in her notice."

"Are you high? Because we both know your mom has a hell of a temper, especially when someone swipes at one of us." Cricket runs a stop sign, and I repeat my question. "Seriously? Are you high?"

She shakes her head. "No. And that used to be a yield sign, thank you very much. I always forget they changed it. I saved the edibles for later."

"Cricket . . ." I don't know what to say to my cousin.

She stops at a red light and turns to me. "We're getting

out of Gable for a couple hours, okay? You've been home for a half second, and yes, some bad shit happened. But I've barely seen you, and you're already plotting your escape. I can't lose you again so soon."

I can feel the guilt trip starting as she turns onto the highway that will take us to High Pines, the next city over the pass, and one that's about double the size of Gable. She didn't tell me where we were going when I got into the van, and I didn't particularly care. *Anywhere but here* seems to be my most desired location at the moment.

"Just give me tonight to change your mind, or at least try to accept the idea of you leaving again."

"Okay. I give in."

Cricket's sunny smile just makes me feel worse about the fact that I'm already mentally repacking my bags and trying to decide where I'm going to go.

"Good! We need cousin time, away from the drama. And when we go back to Gable, we're going to get drunk, because that's pretty much the only way I know how to deal with the thought of you leaving me again. And the thought of Karma being my maid of honor."

And my guilt-o-meter keeps climbing . . .

"Hunter has all these friends coming in for the wedding. He could easily have ten groomsmen. And I'm over here with my sister, who's a cuntcake ninety percent of the time, and my cousin, who can't wait to leave town."

"You know I wish I could stay—"

"Then *stay*. Because you know what my other option is? Marjorie from work. She likes to party. And by party, I mean build shelters in the woods and try to see how long she can go without coming back to civilization. Her armpit hair hits her elbow, and I don't think showers are her friend. The rest of my coworkers are guys, and I'm pretty sure

Hunt would object to having them stand up for me in dresses."

She shoots me a pleading look, as if it's necessary at this point.

"Just give me one night, Whit, and promise me if you have fun tonight, you'll stay another week. Call it a trial basis. We'll sort things out with Mom, and my wedding won't be far off, and you can start the countdown calendar for running away to wherever you want to hide next."

"Fine. I'll stay." What else can I really say to that?

Cricket squeals and reaches over to hug me. The van swerves and I lunge for the steering wheel, but she grabs it before we hit the ditch.

"I'm so glad you see it my way, because I'm actually taking you to get a bridesmaid dress right now so you can't back out."

My jaw drops as I look at my cousin—the one person I didn't think could withhold any information or be remotely sneaky. "You tricked me?"

"It was necessary. Once you've got a dress, you're sticking around for the wedding, and I need you. Like Mom said, you're all that's standing between me and the steam-roller named Mrs. Havalin."

"You win, but only on the condition that I get to pick out something that looks fabulous on me and will look terrible on Karma."

"Yes!" Cricket fist pumps with both hands in the air. "Jesus, take the wheel!"

"Cricket!" I scream as the van hits the rumble strip and veers toward oncoming traffic. Horns blare, but she yanks the wheel back just in time. "Next time, I'm driving."

"Chill out. Eat the candy in the glovebox. You need it way more than I do."

LINCOLN

"YOU PROMISED me you'd play nice with Whitney, man. And now my future mother-in-law is unemployed. What the fuck is going on?" My friend's tone is pissed when I answer his call.

"I didn't know her aunt was going to quit her job until after it was done. I'm going to figure it out."

Hunter releases a long breath. "I'm only getting married once, and I want Cricket to be happy when she walks down the aisle. If her cousin isn't standing up for her, she won't be happy."

"I get it. I'm working on it."

"You better work faster, because if Cricket's last-ditch effort to keep Whitney in town fails, I don't want to have to kick your ass."

I home in on the part of his statement that pertains to Whitney. "What kind of last-ditch effort?"

"She's taking her out to buy her a bridesmaid dress tonight. Probably going to get her hammered afterward so she can't change her mind. I'm going to track them down in a couple hours to make sure they're not getting into too much trouble."

"I'm coming with you."

"Don't take this the wrong way, but you've done enough. I'll talk to you tomorrow."

Hunter doesn't wait for me to respond before he hangs up, and I feel like a shitty friend. I fucked up with Whitney, screwed up her aunt's job, and my best friend is pissed because I put his future bride's happiness in jeopardy.

And I'm going to fix all of it.

Hunter has forgotten one important thing—I'm the CEO of a billion-dollar company, and that's what I do. Fix problems.

First, I'll deal with the easiest one. Jackie's job.

I point my SUV in the direction of the estate. It's time to talk to my mother. She's due for a serving of humble pie.

"I will not apologize. That girl is trash. She's been trash since the day she was born, and she'll die trash."

McKinley glares at me. "Dr. Green said we're supposed to keep her out of stressful situations, and this is what you do first?"

My mother's chin points skyward. "He doesn't care if I die. I'm sure he'd be happy if I did."

The bullshit that passes for truth in this house is one of the biggest reasons I moved out.

"Mother, you know that's not true. I love and respect you, and I know that you understand the magnitude of the problem you've caused for McKinley today."

"She shouldn't be running that hotel to begin with." With

her words, my mother did exactly what I expected her to do —piss my sister off.

"Thanks a lot, Mother," McKinley says with a sigh. "It's great to get your vote of confidence—again."

My mother's chin cuts toward my sister. "You were supposed to find a husband. You failed. Don't blame me for wanting a better life for you than toiling away behind a desk."

"I *like* toiling away behind a desk. I'm a successful CEO. I love my job. I'm happy. I think that means I'm doing just fine." McKinley glances at me. "Lincoln's right. I would like my head of housekeeping back. She's one of the most reliable employees I have."

"I'm not apologizing to her for anything. You can't make me." My mother looks and sounds like a petulant child, with her arms crossed over her chest.

"Maybe your son and daughter can't, but I can, Sylvia." Commodore rolls into the living room with his dog trailing behind, and I have no idea how long he's been listening or how he got here. "I wanted to see for myself that you'd survived your episode. Since you're throwing a tantrum, you must be perfectly fine."

Commodore and my mother have never gotten along, but he is the only person who can control her because he still holds the keys to the kingdom—and keeps a tight grip on the purse strings. It's not hard to conclude that a large part of my mother's bitterness comes from the fact that she expected Commodore to die, leave the family fortune to my father, and then she'd be able to freely spend all the money she married. Expectations have robbed her of any kind of happiness, because life hasn't gone according to her plan.

Instead of sniping back at Commodore, however, my mother goes silent, her eyes blazing with rage as she holds back what is no doubt an impressive volley of vitriol.

"Now, tell me what the hell is going on. Who quit? Is it going to impact the company negatively?" Commodore asks the room in general.

McKinley speaks up. "Jackie Gable. My head of house-keeping. And yes, she's one of the best employees I had, and I'd like to get her back."

Commodore looks at me. "And she quit why, exactly?"

"Mother had some things to say about her niece that she objected to, and she resigned."

The old man's gaze shifts to my mother. "Sylvia, you have an apology to deliver. Feel free to put it in writing if you can't manage to keep a civil tongue around the Gables."

My mother's mouth drops open, and I can't hide my shock at his declaration either.

"Over my dead body," she snaps.

Commodore smiles, but there's no kindness in it. "Since you failed to die once today, I think that's highly unlikely." His gaze sharpens. "As soon as you start interfering with business, you start interfering with me. We both know how that battle will turn out, don't we?"

The old man is savage with her, and while I respect my mother, she does need to be reined in. It's my only chance of repairing the situation I promised to fix.

Commodore maneuvers his chair to face me. "If your mother wants an allowance for next month, she'll deliver the apology in your presence or in writing. If in person, it will not be delivered publicly. Am I understood?"

Mother fumes in silence.

"Anything else, sir?" My question is more of a formality, but Commodore rolls closer to me.

"Yes, as a matter of fact." He stops in front of me and lowers his voice so only I can hear him. "You know what my

196

expectations are. Think very carefully about how you proceed with that Gable girl."

He doesn't wait for a response before spinning around and exiting the room, leaving us all staring after him and no doubt cursing his name.

WHITNEY

The past

COMMODORE RISCOFF SCARED the ever-loving hell out of me, and not just because he was looming over me in the dark. I'd never seen him this close up before, and I'd never wanted to.

His face was lined with wrinkles as he peered down at me. Water beaded off his rain jacket. "I don't want to know what you're doing here, do I, Ms. Gable?"

I didn't know why I wasn't surprised he knew who I was. Commodore Riscoff was akin to the Great and Powerful Oz in this town. He knew everything, and no one questioned him.

I answered as honestly as I could. After all, what more did I have to lose when it came to this family? They'd already taken the farm. And I'd left most of the shreds of my pride on the floor of the cabin where Lincoln essentially called me a whore.

"No, sir. But I suspect you'll find out all the same."

His attention lowered to my bare feet. I'd dropped my shoes somewhere in the woods when I fell, and I wasn't digging for them right now. They could serve as a grave marker for the death of whatever Lincoln and I had thought we had together.

"Do you need a ride home?"

His question surprised me, and even though I wanted to deny it, I told the truth.

"Yes, sir. I would appreciate a ride. It's a long walk in the rain."

His gaze shifted toward the cabin, lights ablaze, and at the long driveway. His lips pressed together as he looked back at me and held out a hand.

"Come on."

I reached out with my uninjured wrist, and he helped me to my feet. Shock numbed the pain of what had happened in the cabin as the Riscoff patriarch helped me into his SUV. Hell must have frozen over. He shut me in the car, and I shivered on the leather seat despite the warm summer night.

Commodore climbed into the driver's seat and looked at me. "Your dad bought a place on the other side of the tracks, correct?"

"Yes, sir."

He backed the SUV onto the road and shifted into drive, heading in the direction that would take us to my parents' house. For the first few minutes, we were both silent, but then he finally spoke.

"You know, Ms. Gable—"

I interrupted him because whatever he had to say, I wasn't sure I could handle hearing it.

"I would really, really appreciate it if you could spare me the lecture about how I'm not good enough for your grandson, and that he's destined for better things and a woman who doesn't have my last name. It's been a shitty night, and he's already made that fact perfectly clear. I have no designs on your grandson. He's safe from me."

The old man glanced at me and returned his attention to the road.

For some reason, I wanted him to know the truth. I wanted him to know that I wasn't some gold digger who was going after his grandson.

"I told him it was a mistake from the moment I found out his last name. He's the one who pushed me to change my mind and give him a chance."

"The boy could charm a rattlesnake if he put his mind to it," the old man remarked, and I nodded in silent agreement. "He's also quite rebellious."

I rolled my eyes at that statement. "So I've heard. Along with the fact that I was his method of getting back at you for making him come home before he planned. That was great to hear, by the way."

"And who did you hear that from?"

"Your son and daughter-in-law." I looked at him. "I hate to say this, sir, but they're both assholes."

Instead of slamming on the brakes and throwing me out of the car, he burst out laughing. The deep rumbles seemed to come straight from his gut.

I studied his profile. Despite his snow-white hair and thick beard, it was obvious to see where Lincoln got his features. His grandfather was probably a good example of exactly what Lincoln would look like in about sixty years.

"You're bold, girl. I respect that. And you're also right. My son didn't follow in my footsteps the way I'd planned."

I sensed that this wasn't something he would normally say, but nothing about tonight was normal. "What do you mean by that?"

"Riscoff men have always been faithful. We've always married not just for money but because our partner makes us better men. My wife was a good woman. Fiercely loyal and as smart as she was beautiful. She was the kind of woman who, in a different day and age, would have been an incredible force to be reckoned with at the bargaining table, mostly because she was so damn stubborn. She kept me on my toes. Made me look forward to waking up every day. That's what I wanted for my son, but that's not what Sylvia turned out to be."

"It sounds like Lincoln's mom doesn't care about any of the things you did either. It sounds like she only cares about him marrying for a name and prestige."

Commodore slowed at a stop sign and his dark brown gaze was pointed. "The idea is to find all of those qualities in one person—rather than needing multiple women to fit the bill. That's where my son went wrong, and I'm not going to let my grandson make the same mistakes."

He didn't have to elaborate for me to understand that I would be one of those mistakes.

"I'm sure you'll do a much better job molding Lincoln in your image now that you've learned from those mistakes."

Instead of continuing through the intersection, he asked me another question. "Is that what you're going to do, Whitney Gable? Learn from your mistakes?"

I turned to stare out the window so he didn't see the tears burning my eyes. "I'm damn sure going to try."

Finally, he hit the gas and we turned. "You would've had an uphill battle if you'd tried to make it work. Everyone would've been against you. His family. Your family."

"Isn't that what life is about? Fighting an uphill battle when it's worth it? And what's more worth it than fighting to be with the person who makes you excited to wake up every day?"

"You sound like a wise girl, despite the fact that you've made some questionable decisions."

"Haven't we all?"

"Indeed we have, Ms. Gable."

We made the rest of the drive in silence, mostly because there was really nothing more to say.

When Commodore pulled up in front of my parents' house, it was completely dark, for which I was thankful. That meant my dad wouldn't be coming out with a gun to try to kill the old man. Lord only knew what he would think if he saw Commodore Riscoff giving me a ride. Undoubtedly, he'd come to the very worst conclusion imaginable.

I reached for the door handle and paused. I needed Lincoln's grandfather to know one more thing. At least, my pride needed him to know.

"I never wanted to be with Lincoln because of his name or your money. Whatever we had, it was despite both of those things."

I didn't wait for an answer before I climbed out of the SUV and headed inside, dripping wet and clutching my burning wrist and my tattered pride.

WHITNEY

Present day

"WHAT IS THIS COLOR, ANYWAY?" Cricket flips up the tag on a gray dress I'm holding. "Mercury? That shit is poisonous, and you're not wearing it at my wedding."

I raise an eyebrow. "I thought I got to pick whatever I wanted."

"Not if it's toxic. You need something like willow, or meadow, or clover." Cricket sweeps her hand toward another section of the rack.

"So, what you really mean is that I can pick anything as long as it's green?"

Her lips quirk up. "You know green would look stunning on you, and I'm a bit of a forest sprite myself." Her brown hair flutters around her shoulders as she twirls.

"How about you pick the color you want me in so I don't screw up your plans, and I'll pick the style."

My cousin's smile grows until I'm afraid she might strain a muscle in her face. "You'd really let me pick?"

"Of course. It's your wedding." To myself I add, *It's not*

the dress that's the hard part; it's sticking around long enough to wear it.

The song playing over the bridal salon stereo changes, and I cringe at the familiar opening bars that I know by heart.

Ricky's voice is going to haunt me forever. I curse my own stupidity every time I hear a song I wrote on the radio. My hard work added up to four albums in ten years, plus who knows how many songs he sold to other people.

Every time I insisted on getting some sort of credit, Ricky talked me out of it by convincing me his career would go to shit if I made it look like he was a poser who couldn't write a song by himself.

Which was the truth.

When I finally put my foot down six months ago, when he started working on his fifth album, he pushed back the recording date and stopped asking for help. This was his game. Wait until there was no more time to extend the deadline, risk breach of contract, and then convince me I was going to ruin both our lives if I didn't do my part like I promised.

But he never made it that far. *And he managed to spend every penny anyway.*

I pretend to flip through the racks, but mostly I'm blocking out the music, feeling like I can't breathe right until the song finally changes.

When it does, to something with a terrible chorus and bridge, I think about all the notebooks of songs I've written that were never sold or recorded. I know I have skills. Ricky's rock-god status cemented that without a doubt. But those songs aren't worth a damn thing sitting where they are, and I'm fresh out of rock stars to sell them to. My other choice is to try to record demos myself . . . which I would never do. My singing voice is strictly for the shower. Besides, Ricky was the one with the great guitar skills. I just knew how to write songs that people loved.

"What about this one?" Cricket interrupts my train of thought when she holds up a bright orange dress that, with my black hair, would make everyone think of Halloween. "It's called persimmon."

When I offer complete silence in response, she laughs. "That was a test. I knew you would hate it, and now I also know what your *no way in hell* face looks like."

A smile tugs at my lips. My cousin knows me well. "Touché."

"At least I'm not making you wear a mushroom." She points to a cluster of brown dresses. "Truffle and morel."

"How about we skip the food colors?"

Cricket turns back to the rack and flips through hanger after hanger. "So that means no apricot, peach, cherry, apple, pear, or guava. Good Lord, what is the obsession with fruit?"

I reach for a dress that's a vivid blue.

"Ohhh, what's that?" Cricket grabs the tag. "Sky. I love that. And it would look stunning on you and only marginally okay on Karma."

There's a high-necked halter option that looks like it would strangle me . . . and then a one-shoulder design that is actually quite pretty.

I hold it up in front of me. "What about this one?"

Cricket claps her hands. "Yes! Try it on!"

The saleswoman, who has been attempting to hover unobtrusively nearby, rushes over at Cricket's exclamation. "This one is a little big for you, but it would only take a week or so to order."

"Good, because we're only three weeks out from the wedding."

When Cricket mentions the date as I step into the fitting

room, it hits me that I've been a terribly shitty cousin because I never asked for her actual wedding date.

Turns out, it's scheduled for the same weekend I married Ricky—when Lincoln's legendary objection happened. I desperately hope that's not a bad omen.

And what's even worse . . . tomorrow is the ten-year anniversary of something I've worked really hard to forget.

WHITNEY

The past

THE HOUSE WAS empty when I walked inside, and for once I was thankful that my dad was likely out drinking, and my mom . . . Well, according to Karma, she was probably out with a man who wasn't my dad.

I shook off the thought. Karma couldn't be right. It had to just be bullshit gossip. I'd borrowed Mom's car a few times that I met Lincoln, so maybe the local gossips had seen *me* and thought I was *her*?

But I'd never been to the Wham Bam Motel.

After my second shower of the evening, I pulled on my comfiest sweats and a ratty old T-shirt and flopped onto my bed with a bag of frozen peas wrapped around my wrist.

Even though I was clean and dry, I felt as bruised and battered as Bouncer, our cat. He walked along the edge of the bed, his tail batting me in the face. He was missing an ear from a fight with another cat in the neighborhood, but he kept coming home, even when I thought he was going to run off for good.

Like I want to do.

Everything that had happened with Lincoln tonight and all his accusations about Ricky came rushing back.

I did send the letter. I couldn't deny that, but Lincoln wouldn't even give me the chance to explain that it wasn't a love note in disguise. It was my way of telling Ricky he was still a shitty songwriter and the only reason he was able to get his big break was because of *me*. Ricky clearly hadn't seen it that way. He'd probably been drunk while he read it, with some bimbo on his lap.

Whatever else he told Lincoln, I had no idea, but it didn't matter.

Lincoln thought I was a cheating whore. *Like mother, like daughter.*

Tears burned the back of my eyes, and I tried to blink them away. I didn't want to cry for him ever again. But just like everything else, I failed at that too. I lifted my knees up to my chest and wrapped my arms around them, rocking back and forth as one by one, tears rolled down my face.

When my phone rang in my purse, I didn't budge. I wasn't answering that thing ever again. There was absolutely no one I wanted to talk to.

Then it rang again. And again. And again.

I finally pulled it out and stared at the screen.

Ricky.

My finger hovered over the button to end the call, but for some stupid reason, I answered.

"What did you tell him?"

"What the hell have you been doing up there, Whit? A Riscoff? Really? They fucking hate your family."

"You no longer have the right to ask me questions like that."

"But, baby, I'm—"

"I don't want to hear it."

I hung up the phone and turned it off. I was done with tonight. Done with everything.

I fell asleep on my bed and didn't wake up until someone pounded on the front door.

LINCOLN

Present day

"WHAT ARE YOU DOING HERE, MAN?"

Hunter rolls down the window of his truck when I pull up and park beside him at Mo's. I'm not too proud to admit that I followed my friend and did a good enough job at it so he wouldn't realize I was tailing him. I just didn't expect to be following him *here*. Back to where it all fucking started. Maybe there's something poetic about that, but I'm certainly not feeling that way right now.

"What do you think I'm doing? I'm here to fix things."

"Look, I get it. You want another shot with the one that got away. Hell, I even respect it. But you gotta back off for now."

"Whitney's aunt has a job at The Gables, if she'll take it. An even better one than she had before."

Hunter's eyebrows hit his hairline. "For real?"

"I've also got an apology from my mother, in writing. If Jackie will accept my mother's apology, McKinley is going to promote her."

"Holy shit. You didn't waste time working that miracle." Hunter leans back in the seat and smiles ruefully. "I should've figured you'd find a way to turn this into a windfall. That's what you do."

"We good?"

"Yeah." He nods. "We're solid."

We climb out of our vehicles and I follow Hunter. I'm glad he's over the idea of kicking my ass—and not just because I don't have many friends I can trust like I trust him.

The tall bastard's head damn near touches the doorway as we walk into the bar. He's built like a brute, even though his mother would like to pretend that their family has never done a day's worth of physical labor. He's got at least a couple of inches and thirty pounds on me, and I'm not small at six feet and two twenty.

"It's been a long time since I've been here," I say as my shoes crush peanut shells on the cement floor.

"It's Cricket's favorite. For what reason, I'll never know."

Mo's hasn't changed at all since the one and only other time I've been here. It's crazy how sometimes it only takes doing something different once to change the entire course of your life.

All I can hope is that tonight changes it for the better.

My eyes adjust to the dim lighting, and it takes me all of three seconds to spot Whitney. Her dark hair swings over her shoulder the moment Cricket squeals when she sees Hunter, jumping up and dodging tall tables and the people sitting at them to get to him.

Whitney's blue gaze lands on me, and everyone else in the room may as well have gone up in smoke. She stares at me for long moments without blinking, and I'd give anything to know what the hell she's thinking.

Is she remembering that night we met? I would give just

about any fucking thing to have tonight end the same way that one did.

I study Whitney's face as she takes her time looking me over. Her expression isn't angry. She isn't running in the other direction.

Maybe . . . maybe I do have a chance to fix this.

Cricket rushes past me, probably to throw herself at Hunter, and I walk toward Whitney slowly, as if she's an animal I'm trying not to spook. She doesn't run. She doesn't even break eye contact.

When I stop in front of her, an apology is the first thing out of my mouth. "I'm sorry."

"I'm sorry, too."

Her reply stuns me. "For what?"

"Because tomorrow . . ."

When she pauses, a pang stabs me in the chest because I know exactly what she's going to say. I can't believe I managed to forget this year. Whitney opens her mouth to keep speaking, but a redheaded biker chick stops beside her.

"I know who you are. Thought I was dreaming. But you're the bitch who killed Ricky Rango." She waves to a guy in a black leather vest. "Bruno. It's her! Whitney Rango!"

For fuck's sake.

The woman gets in Whitney's face, and I step around her and move Whitney behind me without touching the woman.

"I'm going to ask you once to leave her alone—"

Bruno barrels toward me. "Don't you get in her face, motherfucker. That's my sister."

Fucking hell.

The last thing I want to do is get into a bar fight with a biker, but apparently fights are the only reason I come to Mo's. That, and to see Whitney Gable.

The woman jabs her finger into my chest. "I don't give a shit about you, asshole. My beef's with her. She killed the legend. She should be in jail for what she did to him. So, get the fuck out of my way because I'm gonna kick her fucking ass."

Whitney moves back, and I step away from the woman. "We're leaving."

Bruno shoves his sister behind him. "I got this."

His fist comes flying toward my face. I block the first punch, conscious of the press of Whitney's body against my back.

The woman comes charging toward my side, no doubt to get to Whitney, but Cricket grabs her arm and spins her around.

"Not today, bitch. That's my cousin."

Glancing at Cricket costs me. Knuckles connect with my chin, and my head snaps sideways.

Instinct kicks in as adrenaline dumps into my system. I retaliate with a combination. The biker's head rocks back and he crashes into a tall table. The two women sitting at it screech as their drinks go flying, and he hits the floor.

Hunter lifts Cricket away from the woman who started this shit show, and Cricket uses the leverage to kick out and catch the redhead in the chest. Bruno's sister flies backward to land on her ass in front of a group of bikers before Hunter carries Cricket out the front. The bikers stand, their attention split between Hunter and me, and it's time to go.

I throw an arm around Whitney and hustle her out the back door just like I did last time.

WHITNEY

I TRIP on the step behind Mo's, and Lincoln picks me up and jogs toward a Range Rover parked around the side. The lights flash, and he sets me down next to the passenger door before yanking it open.

"Get in."

I scramble into the SUV and slam the door shut as he rounds the hood. Out the window, Hunter has Cricket over his shoulder as he heads for his truck. Cricket smacks his ass with every step.

Even that comical sight can't stop reality from intruding and killing every hint of my buzz.

I'll never get past what happened. Never. I'll always be the woman who killed Ricky Rango, even though I didn't do it.

All I wanted was a divorce.

Bikers spill out around the side of the bar as Lincoln throws the Range Rover into reverse.

"As much as I don't mind defending your honor, we're not coming back to Mo's. That place is—"

"Cursed? Like me?" I laugh, but there's not a bit of humor in it.

"You're not cursed."

A beer bottle hits the back window of the SUV, and I flinch before jerking around to watch as Lincoln floors it. Hunter does the same, and his spinning tires shower the bikers with gravel. As they take cover, we haul ass out of the parking lot.

"I'm so sorry. I'd offer to pay for the damage, but I don't know if I can afford to fix a Range Rover."

My words bring forth a wave of humiliation. *My life is a joke. I'll never outrun my past. I'm destined to repeat it over and over.*

I stare out the side mirror as the lights of Mo's disappear behind us.

"Don't worry about it."

Lincoln checks the rearview mirror, and I'm hoping no one is coming after us. I don't see headlights, so maybe they aren't going to try to track us down.

When we're safely away, he looks to me. "Are you okay?"

I swallow and nod. Physically, anyway. Emotionally, I'm a hot freaking mess.

It doesn't matter where I go or what I do, everything I touch turns to shit. I can't do anything without everything going wrong.

The voices in my head won't let me forget how much of a complete and utter failure I am on every level. A bad daughter. A worthless sister. A terrible cousin. A shitty niece. A crappy wife. I'll never escape it.

"It'll never stop. Ever," I whisper, wanting to close myself off and wallow in self-pity. "I just need to go somewhere no one knows my name and become a hermit."

"That's not going to happen. You're not running again. This is your home. Stand your ground."

I choke out a humorless laugh. "Yeah, like it's that easy."

Lincoln turns onto a road that I know damn well doesn't go back to Gable.

"Where are we going?"

"My place."

My shoulders slump in the seat, and the feeling of defeat is overwhelming. "I can't take another round of the past repeating itself tonight. It'd be better if you just take me back to Jackie's."

Lincoln glances at me. "Do you really want to go sleep in a shed tonight and tear yourself to pieces about what happened at the bar?"

He has a point. I also hate that he knows me well enough to predict what I would do.

"No," I whisper. "I just want to forget all of it."

"Then leave it all behind for a few hours."

His offer is tempting.

"And what do you expect in return?" I ask because in my world, nothing comes without strings attached.

Lincoln slows down and pulls over to the side of the road. He throws the Range Rover into park. "Are you really asking me that?"

I swallow. Based on the ticking of his jaw, it's clear I've pissed him off. "You know what I mean. You want things from me that I don't know if I can give."

"You have my word that absolutely nothing happens tonight, or *ever*, between us that you don't want just as much as I do. You know me better than that."

I hate that I know this man and yet feel like I don't know him all at the same time.

He squeezes the steering wheel and turns to face me. "I need to tell you something else. Full disclosure, but not because I'm trying to sway your decision."

Apprehensive chills work their way through my body. "What?"

"Your aunt is getting an apology from my mother and a promotion from my sister, if she'll accept them."

I stare at him, my mouth dropping open. "Are you serious?"

"Yes."

I turn to look out the windshield into the dark of night. He's already fixed one of the biggest things that has been weighing on me. "I don't know what to say."

"You don't have to say anything. I just wanted you to know, but also . . . there are no strings. You can tell me to turn around right now and take you home, and the offer still stands. Whatever happens between you and me has absolutely nothing to do with that."

"And yet your timing of telling me is so convenient." The skepticism in my voice is clear.

Lincoln's brows dive together. "Yeah, it is. I didn't want you to spend the rest of the night thinking you fucked up your aunt's life by coming home."

"Oh." My reply is quiet.

"You can think I'm the bad guy all you want, Blue. Sometimes I am. There are plenty of things I won't hesitate to use to my advantage to get what I want from you, but I won't manipulate you through your family. I'm above that."

For some reason, I actually believe him. Maybe because he's being honest about his intentions.

"Then I guess I should thank you." It feels strange to say the words, but I mean them.

"You don't need to thank me. It was my mother's fault to begin with. She never should've said those things to you."

"She'll always hate me." I look out the window as shame pools in my belly about what happened ten years ago. Even if

217

it wasn't my fault, I still carry the burden of it on my soul. "You should hate me too."

Lincoln waits until I turn back toward him to speak. His expression is completely solemn. "I don't hate you. I never have. I never could. You didn't do it, and neither did I. I've moved on. I think it's time for you to let go too."

LINCOLN

· *The past*

AS SOON AS I pulled my head out of my ass and realized what the fuck I'd done, I ran outside. Whitney was gone. I ran barefoot down the gravel drive, but there was no sign of her.

Fuck.

She'd run off once before and hitched a ride, but that was daylight. Now it was fucking raining, pitch black, and anyone could have picked her up.

"Fuck!" I roared at the storming sky, cursing my temper and how I let Rango get to me.

Regardless of whether Whitney actually did what he said, I shouldn't have thrown her out. I regretted it almost as soon as she walked out the door.

But not soon enough.

I ran back up the driveway, gravel biting at the soles of my feet as the rain soaked me through.

What kind of piece of shit throws a woman out in the middle of the night in the rain? Me.

I had to make sure she got home okay. I'd never be able to live with myself if something happened to her.

I grabbed my phone, dialing her number, but it went to voice mail with no answer. Palming my keys, I rushed back out of the cabin, the door slamming behind me.

I have to get to her.

I fishtailed out of the driveway, my tires breaking loose on the slick road. I almost lost control of the truck, but I wrenched it back in the direction I needed to go.

Branches swayed as the wind picked up and I navigated down the winding mountain roads. I hadn't caught up to any taillights, and I searched the sides of the road for a lone woman walking.

I found nothing. I called her again and again, but it kept going to voice mail.

It took me almost thirty minutes to pull up in front of Whitney's parents' house, but it was completely dark.

Headlights blinded me as another car flew down the street and whipped into the driveway. Whitney's aunt, the one who my mother fired, jumped out of a car and ran to the door, soaking wet. She pounded on it like a crazy woman.

Fuck. In the pit of my stomach, I knew something wasn't right.

I climbed out of my car, and Jackie turned when I slammed my door.

"Get the hell out of here, kid."

"No, I need to see Whitney. I need to make sure she's all right."

"She's never going to be all right again." Jackie's voice was ragged. "You shouldn't be here." She turned and pounded on the door again as her shoulders shook.

Something unsettling twisted in the pit of my stomach.

My phone vibrated, and I looked down. *Mother.*

"What the fuck is going on?"

Jackie glanced over her shoulder and looked down at my phone. "You should answer that."

WHITNEY

Present day

WE PASS THE RESORT, and then the estate. Another mile beyond it, Lincoln approaches a third gate that I've never seen before. It's not as ornate as the black wrought iron and gold accents of the resort and the estate. It's more understated, but every bit as forbidding.

It doesn't take a genius to figure out that this is Lincoln's house, and my decision to come here already feels like the wrong one.

"I should've had you take me home," I whisper as the gates swing open.

"I want you here," he replies as he drives through them. "But if you want me to take you back to your aunt's, I will."

As he navigates the Range Rover up the long driveway, we disappear into dense forest dotted with lights. A brighter glow comes from farther beyond, and when we round the last bend, I finally see the house.

It's not a gargantuan mansion or an over-the-top monstrosity.

No, of course not. Because this is Lincoln we're talking about. Instead, it's just fucking *perfect.*

For some reason, that puts me over the edge.

"Okay, then take me home."

Lincoln turns to face me. "Why? What's wrong?"

"I can't do this. Not here. Not anywhere so fucking perfect. You don't get it!"

"Get what, Whitney?"

I spin to face him. "You don't get what it's like to never be able to do anything right! For everything you try to fix to go horribly wrong instead. I came home because Cricket begged me and I didn't have anywhere else to go. But instead of making her wedding dreams come true, I've made everything worse. I'm a fuckup. A joke. The goddamned black widow who killed someone by trying to divorce him!"

Tears stream down my face, and I don't care if I sound completely and utterly hysterical.

"Right now, I can't be rational. I can't be reasonable. And I can't keep having your perfect fucking life shoved in my face to show me just how screwed up mine is!"

Instead of backing out of the driveway, Lincoln kills the engine, unbuckles his seat belt, and opens his door.

"Take me home," I tell him, my voice creeping toward shrill.

He doesn't listen. He rounds the hood and opens the passenger door.

I slap at his hands as he unbuckles my seat belt. "I want to go home! You said you'd take me home."

But he doesn't stop. He lifts me out of the SUV and carries me toward his perfect freaking house while I beat on his shoulders. Then he puts me down right in front of the door.

"Shut up for two fucking seconds and listen to what I

have to say." He points at the glass, and I can see straight through to the darkness on the other side of the floor-to-ceiling windows that must make up the back of the house. "You see that?"

"What do you want me to see? It's a perfect fucking house to go with your perfect fucking life!"

"Wrong. It's just a goddamned house. It has no meaning beyond walls and windows and doors. There's no laughter. No family. No love. Only wood and glass and rock that means absolutely fucking *nothing* in the grand scheme of things."

I blink twice as I try to comprehend the point he's making.

"You think your life is so fucking screwed up? Try having everything you could ever want but never being happy. Never having someone you can trust to love and share it with. You think my life is so fucking perfect? Well, it's not, Whitney. Perfection walked out of my life the day you married another man."

We stand in front of each other, our chests heaving, and my tears fall harder.

"So I ruined your life too?" I snuffle in a sob, and I'm close to full-on bawling.

LINCOLN

I swear to God, no matter what I say to this woman, I'm destined to fuck it up.

"No. Fuck no." I wrap my arms around her and yank her into my chest, letting her tears soak my shirt. "I did that all by myself."

"Then—"

She sniffles, and I hug her harder.

"What I meant is that just because something looks perfect from the outside doesn't mean it is, and the things that look like a complete disaster are sometimes better than we could ever imagine." I pull back, and she lifts her chin to meet my gaze. Her blue eyes shine with tears, and just like it always has, it guts me to see her cry.

"We've always thrived in the middle of chaos. In the middle of adversity. That's where you and I excel. All you have to do is give me another chance, and we can make this work. I swear to you we can."

"How can you think it would end any differently than in some kind of fiery disaster, with us running in opposite directions, and the world burning down around our ears?"

I cup her chin and stare into her eyes. "Because this time I'm not giving up. Because with you and me against the world, we can't lose."

When my lips touch hers, everything else falls away, and the Whitney I remember comes to life in my arms.

I fumble for my door handle, thankful that my thumbprint opens it, and I pull her inside and pin her against the door.

Whitney claws at my shoulders even as she says against my lips, "We shouldn't do this. This is a terrible idea. I'm cursed. I swear I am."

"Shut up, Blue. I'm a hell of a lot more worried about you kissing me than cursing me."

I lift her into my arms and carry her to my bed. The bed where I've never had another woman. The bed where I've only ever wanted *this* woman.

I've waited years for another chance. I'm not going to fuck it up.

Not this time.

WHITNEY

I KNOW it's a bad idea. I know that I should stick to my guns and make him take me home, but sometimes, after life shovels so much shit in your direction, you just want one good thing.

Lincoln's always been paradise and disaster wrapped in a beautiful package I can't resist. Tonight, I'm willing to do anything to have one more chance to taste paradise. The rest of the world can wait until tomorrow.

Tonight is ours.

As he carries me into his bedroom, I don't bother to look at the house. It doesn't matter. He's right. It's only walls and windows and doors. None of it means anything. I know all about living a life that looked perfect from the outside, but was completely hollow.

The only thing that matters is Lincoln and me, and shutting up the voices in my head that won't let me forget how much of a failure I am.

When he lays me down on the smooth coverlet, the voices finally go silent. The only thing left in my brain is Lincoln.

"I've waited ten years for this moment. I'm going to take my time."

My entire body shivers as he reaches for the hem of his T-shirt and pulls it over his head, revealing a stomach that's still flat and hard. His rounded pecs and shoulders seem even broader and thicker than I remember, but his eyes are still the same. The hazel flashes with heat as he stares down at me before coming toward the bed, his jeans still on. He kneels between my legs and kisses me like he'd die if he had to wait another moment to taste my lips. The same way he always kissed me.

My body heats as he trails his mouth along my chin, skimming my ear, and then down my throat.

"Please . . ." I don't even know what I want, but I'm already begging for whatever he'll give me.

"Shhh. Let me explore."

The strap of my tank slides down my shoulder, and he covers every inch of my bare skin with his lips, tasting, teasing, and testing my control.

I lose myself in him, in the feel of his skin, in the scent that's new but somehow familiar all at the same time.

He peels my tank down my body to reveal my hard nipples straining against the sheer lace of my bra. I may not have left LA with much, but I did bring all my nice underwear, and for the first time, I thank my lucky stars for that.

Lincoln sucks in a breath. "Fuck, you're beautiful. So fucking beautiful."

He skims a thumb over the bud of my nipple, and I arch toward him.

"You want my lips here?"

"Yes."

He replaces his thumb with his mouth and sucks the hardened tip inside.

Heat dumps into my veins as he scrapes it along his teeth. I lift my hips, needing pressure. Lincoln knows what I want, and his free hand slides between us to cup me between my legs.

I buck against his hand, wishing my clothes were already off. "More."

He lifts his head from my breast. "Greedy girl."

Lincoln doesn't realize that I'm only this way for him. Never for anyone else. Maybe someday I'll tell him that, but tonight, I just want to revel in the things only he can make me feel.

He moves his hand to tug at the button of my shorts. He stands to pull them off, and I shimmy to help them along.

Lincoln stands above me, the bulge in his jeans impossible to miss as he stares down at my body like he's cataloging every inch.

Insecurities about how much my body has changed creep in, but he banishes them.

"I don't know how it's possible, but you're even more beautiful than you were before. You were a girl then. Now you're a goddess, and I'm going to worship you."

He kneels on the floor, his head between my legs, and this time his mouth moves over my center. His hot breath teases me through the lace of my panties, and I grip his hair in my hands.

He drags his fingers along the fabric until my wetness soaks the barrier between us, and he finally pushes it aside. His tongue skims my slick heat, gliding along the edges of my bare lips until I want to scream for him to give me what I need.

But he already knows what I need. Lincoln closes his mouth over my clit and sucks hard as he pushes a finger inside me.

Just like that . . . I. Am. Done.

I buck against his mouth, his name on my lips as I come harder than I have since the last time he touched me. But once isn't enough. Lincoln's lips and teeth and tongue destroy me until I'm gasping for air and my throat feels raw. Only then does he rise and move up my body, pressing kisses to my skin as he goes.

"So fucking sweet," he whispers.

I fumble between us for the button on his jeans and shove them over his hips. His cock bobs free, and I wrap my hand around his thick length.

"Fuck, Blue. *Fuck*."

"Please, Lincoln. Please. I need you." I've always needed him. I always will need him. It's part of me that will never go away.

He rolls off the bed and kicks off his jeans and briefs before pulling a condom out of the nightstand. I wonder how many women he's had here, but I don't ask. I don't want to know.

My thought must be completely transparent, though, because he replies to my unspoken question.

"Only you. No other woman has ever been in my bed."

He rolls on the condom, and when he moves back between my legs, everything feels so *perfect*.

Maybe Lincoln is right. Maybe we can do this. Maybe we don't just have tonight. Maybe we could have forever.

When he pushes inside me, I forget to care about anything but how he makes me feel.

LINCOLN

SLIDING into Whitney is like coming home. She's perfection wrapped in thorns, but the reward is so incredible, you're willing to risk the sting.

I know I won't last long in the tight heat of her body, but I will not fucking come until she does one more time. I take my time, savoring every thrust and pump, pretending this could be the last time, even as I tell myself it can't be.

Her inner muscles flutter around my cock, telling me she's close. Her breathy little sighs turn into moans as my balls tighten, and I know I don't have long.

When she clamps down on me and screams my name, I let go, unleashing the most intense orgasm I've had since her.

No one can compare to Whitney. Not then. Not ever. And this time, she's mine for good.

After we clean up, I wrap my arms around her and hold her for hours before falling asleep. Every moment feels precious when you know what it's like to lose the person who matters most.

For some reason, with Whitney, every time we're together feels like time is always moving too fast. Always running out.

I fight sleep, not wanting to close my eyes, but I eventually succumb.

WHITNEY

THE PILLOWCASE FEELS like silk against my skin—something I used to be accustomed to, but I'm not anymore and never will be again. My eyes flick open and I look around. One wall is completely glass, and the view beyond it is absolutely breathtaking.

Outside, dark gray walls of rock are topped with tall pines and cedars. At the base of the gorge, the river rushes over rapids, and the sight is so incredible, I swear I can hear the churning water.

Where the hell am I?

I look down and realize I'm naked. The ache between my thighs reminds me of exactly what happened last night.

A glance at the pillow beside the one I woke up on tells me that I didn't imagine falling asleep wrapped in Lincoln's arms.

That was real. Everything was real.

For a moment, I wonder if he left me here, but I know he hasn't.

I can't be within a hundred yards of Lincoln Riscoff and not feel his presence. It's something visceral I've never been able to shake. He's been in my blood from that first night, and I've never been able to get him out.

I spy my tank and shorts on the floor and snatch them up. Dropping the sheet, I dress before padding toward the window to stare for long moments.

It's the most awe-inspiring sight I've ever seen. Even the view from The Gables can't top it. It's so perfectly Lincoln.

The rushing water of the river also reminds me of what day it is.

How has it been ten years?

WHITNEY

The past

THE POUNDING WOULDN'T STOP, and even the pillow over my head couldn't drown it out. I jumped out of bed and hurried down the stairs, expecting to see my dad out front without his keys.

But when I opened the door, I was absolutely wrong.

Jackie's face was haggard as she stood in front of the door, soaked from the rain. Lincoln was behind her, his phone to his ear.

Who is he calling? Me? But he didn't hang up immediately.

"What the hell is going on?" I asked, and my aunt wrapped her fingers around my wrist and tugged toward her.

"You need to come with me, Whit. Right now. We have to go to the hospital."

My stomach twisted into an unholy knot as she pulled me outside. The wind whipped my black hair in every direction as the rain pelted my thin shirt. My gaze cut back to Lincoln as his expression turned into a mask of horror.

"What happened? Someone tell me. Now."

Jackie's head bowed and she hauled in a ragged breath. Lincoln lowered the phone, his face pale, and he seemed almost frozen in shock.

"Jesus fucking Christ," he whispered, and my heart thundered, spurred on by fear.

"Please, tell me."

My aunt yanked me against her chest and wrapped her arms around me. "I'm so sorry, Whit. There's been a terrible accident. We have to go to the hospital now."

Tremors racked my body as she pulled back. "What happened?" My plea came out raw and ragged, but Jackie looked at Lincoln.

"They told you?"

He nodded, lifting a hand to his face. "Yeah." His voice sounded as hoarse as mine. "I'll follow you to the hospital."

His hazel gaze dragged over my face, and his shattered expression shredded me.

"What happened?" I screamed the question.

Lincoln swallowed. "I'm so sorry, Whitney."

LINCOLN

Present day

"Pretty awesome view, isn't it?"

I stand in the doorway of my bedroom, holding a cup of coffee as I watch Whitney stare out the window. She turns to face me, her expression bleak.

"I'm so sorry, Lincoln."

I already know why she's sorry, but she shouldn't be. I move toward her, pausing at the nightstand to leave the coffee I brought for her.

"Neither of us could've stopped what happened that night. It's been ten years. It's time to let go of the past. Time to move on. Start over." I wrap an arm around her, and she curls into my chest. "I think today is the perfect time for a new beginning. What about you?"

She looks up at me with those big blue eyes and nods. "I think you're right. It's time to start over. Leave the past behind us."

Thank God. Finally.

I lower my lips to kiss her forehead and hold her for long moments as we stare out the window together. Today may be a hard day for both of us, but it's easier with Whitney in my arms. I feel like what I said last night is true.

With Whitney and me together against the world, we can't lose.

Out in the living room, Whitney's phone rings, and she pulls back. "My aunt probably wonders what the hell happened to me last night. I told her I'd be coming home late."

I follow her into the kitchen, and my phone vibrates on the counter.

Four missed calls and three texts? In five minutes? What the hell?

Almost on instinct, my heart rate picks up as I open a text from my sister first.

MCKINLEY: You need to answer your phone. The shit has hit the fan.

A text from my lawyer is next.

JOHNSON: We have a serious problem.

From my brother.

HARRISON: I hope you didn't fuck her again, because she just fucked you even harder.

"What the hell?" I whisper as I click on the link to the newspaper article Harrison sent. The headline knocks me back on my heels.

RICKY RANGO'S ESTATE CLAIMS HE WAS THE TRUE RISCOFF HEIR

What. The. Fuck.

I turn and look at Whitney. "What have you done?"

WHITNEY AND LINCOLN'S **story continues in Guilty as Sin.**

ALSO BY MEGHAN MARCH

Sin Trilogy

Richer Than Sin

Guilty As Sin

Reveling In Sin

Mount Trilogy:

Ruthless King

Defiant Queen

Sinful Empire

Savage Trilogy

Savage Prince

Iron Princess

Rogue Royalty

Beneath Series:

Beneath This Mask

Beneath This Ink

Beneath These Chains

Beneath These Scars

Beneath These Lies

Beneath These Shadows

Beneath The Truth

DIRTY BILLIONAIRE TRILOGY:

Dirty Billionaire

Dirty Pleasures

Dirty Together

DIRTY GIRL DUET:

Dirty Girl

Dirty Love

REAL DUET:

Real Good Man

Real Good Love

REAL DIRTY DUET:

Real Dirty

Real Sexy

FLASH BANG SERIES:

Flash Bang

Hard Charger

STANDALONES:

Take Me Back

Bad Judgment

ABOUT THE AUTHOR

Meghan March has been known to wear camo face paint and tromp around in the woods wearing mud-covered boots, all while sporting a perfect manicure. She's also impulsive, easily entertained, and absolutely unapologetic about the fact that she loves to read and write smut.

Her past lives include slinging auto parts, selling lingerie, making custom jewelry, and practicing corporate law. Writing books about dirty-talking alpha males and the strong, sassy women who bring them to their knees is by far the most fabulous job she's ever had.

She would love to hear from you. Connect with her at:

Website:
www.meghanmarch.com
Facebook:
www.facebook.com/MeghanMarchAuthor
Twitter:
www.twitter.com/meghan_march
Instagram:
www.instagram.com/meghanmarch

CPSIA information can be obtained
at www.ICGtesting.com
Printed in the USA
LVHW01s1757130918
590068LV00003B/530/P

9 781943 796199